To be honest, I hadn't given the whole "soldier" concept much thought. I still can't fathom that I'd been created with the singular purpose of fighting some unknown enemy. My focus has been on saving my sisters. A blur of war images flashes through my mind. It's not somewhere I want to be. I shudder.

PRAISE FOR THE WORKS OF SHARON M. JOHNSTON

"...authors like Sharon M. Johnston keep the genre (New Adult) from getting stale by taking a creative bent and exploring overlapping elements."

- LIBRARY JOURNAL

"This story by Sharon M Johnston will tug at your heart strings and leave you raw, and yet wanting desperately to read more!"

- READERS' FAVORITE

"As Mishca's life unfolds, you pick up on a few eyebrow raises. *Divided* is an intriguing story that left me curious with what would be happening next."

- ECLIPSE REVIEWS

"*Divided* is a fast-paced adventure filled with mystery, romance, action, and humor. Mishca and Ryder rank up there with my favorite heroines and heroes ever! Sharon M. Johnston is an author to watch out for."

- *USA Today* & *New York Times* bestselling author, WENDY HIGGINS.

By Sharon M. Johnston

DIVIDED

SHATTERED

Coming Soon
DIRTY RAINBOW

Anthologies
THE BASICS OF LIFE

WORDS WITH HEART

SHARON M. JOHNSTON

SHATTERED

AN OPEN HEART NOVEL

Book Two

CITY OWL
PRESS

This book is a work of fiction. Names, characters, places, and incidents either are products of the author's imagination or are used fictitiously. Any resemblance to actual events or locales or persons, living or dead, is entirely coincidental and not intended by the author.

SHATTERED
An Open Heart Novel: Book Two

CITY OWL PRESS
www.cityowlpress.com

Cover Design by Tina Moss. All stock photos licensed appropriately.

For information on subsidiary rights, please contact the publisher at info@cityowlpress.com.

Print Edition ISBN: 978-1-944728-06-9

Digital Edition ISBN: 978-1-519937-89-6

Printed in the United States of America

To Mum,

Thanks for raising me in a home that encouraged

creativity and embraced weirdness.

- Sharon

PROLOGUE

RYDER

A LOT OF PEOPLE THINK I dreamed it—and yes, I have dreamed about it a lot—but I know it happened. It was real. I can still remember it. Clearly. Too clearly. The day my mother gave me up. It is etched in my brain.

Mist hovers in the air around us, and as Mum rushes through the city night, bits cling to our clothes, dampening us both. She holds me close to her. So close that I am snuggled into her silk dress. Each hurried step jostles me. She smells like strawberries and freshly cut grass mingled together.

For some reason I cannot explain, the night sky, lit by streetlights, feels foreign to me. The cool air seeps through the bundle of blankets. I fidget, longing for the warmth of home. Someone speaks to Mum, but I miss the words before we head inside a house.

Normally I feel safe in my mother's arms, but today fear rolls off her and infects me. We are in a strange place, in a room that is not mine. Outside, turmoil reigns. Footsteps thud and raised voices call out in protest. Mum places me into a crib so that I face a slowly spinning mobile embellished with stars and set against a stark white ceiling.

I reach for her. She has soft skin with a peaches-and-cream complexion and long thin blond hair that falls onto my face as she leans forward to whisper to me.

"My darling child," her lips are like pink rose petals in the morning dew, "it is time for you to go and join your new family. They can give you what I cannot, shelter and protection. But you must change to be accepted with them. Do not be like me. Be like them and you will be safe."

Two crystal tears roll down from each of her blue eyes, sliding over her cheeks and falling onto my face.

The door to the room opens. "We have to go," a male voice says. "There was…a problem."

She kisses me and then leaves me. The emptiness of the room consumes me. I cry like I had never cried before, and it feels like I will never stop being filled with sorrow.

I remember nothing else until the normal memories that one gets as they grow come to me. Snippets and fragments of my developmental years only.

I know I never saw her again after that night. But that is all I have ever wanted. For so long, I was losing faith that I would find my mum.

Until now.

CHAPTER 1

MISHCA

MY HANDS GRIP THE steering wheel so tight my knuckles resemble mini snow-capped mountains. I could drive under the truck 200 meters ahead in the opposite lane and end it all. It would be easy. Accelerate, yank the wheel, and then nothingness. The scenario plays through my mind so vividly I actual wince.

Suck it up, soldier. This pity party is over.

I shake my head as though that will make the intrusive thoughts dissipate. The best thing might be to think of nothing at all. Dwelling on the fact that people want to kill my sisters, remembering how I stuffed everything with Ryder, thinking about Isobel and how I'm her incarnate, picturing Colin. Ah crap, now I'm on Colin.

I want to travel back in time and bitch-slap past-me for ever believing that Imogene's love for Colin was my own. Part of me is furious with my original for passing on her insanely passionate feelings for my former university professor. The other part of me is furious with Colin for not realizing that I was his soul mate's duplicate. Being a clone sucks ass.

I distract my chaotic mind with loud music and focus on the road. The further I drive, the more the houses decrease and the trees increase. I slow down as a mailbox shaped like a shell appears ahead, sitting in front of a driveway hedged by masses of giant gums. I turn in and continue down the path surrounded by shadows and trees. The sunlight throws a glare through my windshield as the car comes into the clearing. A large two-story home made of wood with a large veranda sits nestled in the middle.

Killing the ignition on Mum's car with a gentle flick of my wrist, I sit still for a moment. Betsy is too conspicuous for me to be driving around now. The soldier side of me has a red alert meltdown whenever I contemplate driving my hot pink car. My fists clench and unclench, leaving fingernail crescent marks in my palms. The frustrated sister part of me wants to grab the wheel, shake it, and shout. Explaining that to Mum is the only thing that stops me.

No putting this off any longer. Go in there and get your best friend back. Grovel if necessary.

Despite the urge to avoid any potential conflict and flee, I force myself from the car and make my way to the front door. My hand lifts to knock as the door swings open. Nerissa's brother Dorian has the back of his head to me while he yells up the hallway, "Mum, do you need me to bring anything back from the shops?"

A faint "no" floats back to us. My feet and mouth refuse to move. Dorian crashes into me as he dashes through the door.

"Omph." We fall in a pile; unfortunately, he lands on top. His large frame crushes me. His blue eyes are cloudy grey today.

"Mishca?" He jumps off me and then offers a hand up. "Are you okay?"

I brush at my clothes. "Yeah, I'm fine."

"That's not what I mean." His stare pierces me. The overprotective vibe I got from him that night when we all went to the Bowl has disappeared, and I'm left wondering why. "You've been through some heavy stuff this year. Are you *okay*?"

My stomach swirls with anxiety like there's a mini black hole wanting to suck me inside. *How could she tell him I'm a clone?* I know Dorian and Nerissa are close, but this isn't her secret to tell.

Inside, the hard-arse me and the shit-scared me battle for control. The soldier wins. "As best as could be expected."

I can't bring myself to verbalize the reality aloud.

Dorian gives me a half smile. "Well, it totally wasn't cool for that Colin dude to treat you like that." I flinch at the name of my original's soul mate, and my almost-lover. Then, a weight on my shoulders lightens. He doesn't know what I am. He glances up the hallway.

"Nerissa will be so happy to see you. She's missed you so much." So I've somehow managed to pass the are-you-good-enough-to-be-friends-with-my-sister test, despite the wall I put up in my mini-melt down. He sticks his head inside and yells, "Hey, nerd-burger! Mishca's here."

The thumping of feet follows his words. *How can someone so light make so much noise?* A squeal escapes Nerissa when she sees me. She's on me in a couple of strides. I hug her back, but let go at her wince.

"Let's go out the back." She clutches my hand and drags me down the hall and through the house, only letting me go once we're outside. When we've settled under the pergola beside their large lagoon, Nerissa stares at me, the pain in her eyes. "I've missed you."

She could've said much worse.

"I know." I turn away. I can't keep my gaze on her without my heart wanting to shatter into a million pieces.

"How's everything going?"

I flex my fingers. "Better. I know I'm the worst," I pause and have to force the words to release from their captivity, "person in the world for ignoring your calls and messages straight after. And for going AWOL. I couldn't face you...or anyone. I needed some time."

"It's okay." The sincerity in her eyes compounds my guilt.

"Mom and Dad were the hardest. I'm still so scared they're going to find out." I run a hand through my hair. "How could they want me if they know the truth?"

She squeezes my hand. "Give them a little more credit than that. Do you think they'd be scared off by how you were born?"

Created, I correct her silently. An image of that night

and the lab full of half-made humans flashes through my mind. I never inspected them close enough to see if they were more versions of Imogene and Finlay's day or new test subjects altogether.

"Everybody's got something about them, some secret that they never want to see the light of day."

"Oh yeah?" I challenge. "What's yours?"

"You know mine," Nerissa replies, looking to her left.

"Right, how goes the wedding plans?"

"Faster than I'd like." She recrosses her legs and taps her fingers against her thigh in a silent beat.

A small warning flares up at the back of my mind. "Do you love Dylan, or are you with him for your parents?"

She doesn't reply straight away. *Mishca, how could you bring that up? You're such a schmuck.*

"Yeah, I love the big lout. I guess we're lucky that it's not a situation where we're strangers when it's our time to tie the knot."

"So that's it?" I ask, scrunching my brows. "You've got an arranged marriage? I thought there might have been something else. Something more...serious."

Her eyes won't meet mine again. This time she glances to her right, shaking her head. "Yeah, that's my big secret." She scratches her nose and tries to smile, but only her lips move. I know for certain Nerissa is lying to me. I don't interrogate her, despite the urge. She embraces me. "I don't care about any of that stuff with you. You have to believe me."

"I know that now. I'm sorry I didn't give you more

credit." I give her an extra squeeze, careful not to be too hard.

Her words and body language run through my thoughts. She's not lying about being betrothed to Dylan. Her movements betrayed her nervousness. Looking to her left means she was recalling something real and telling me the truth. But when she replied that her arranged marriage was her big secret she looked to her right, scratched her nose, and reinforced my question. *Hold up, I'm a human lie detector too?*

"I'm glad you've been in contact with Ryder. He was so worried. You know he called me a zillion times."

I almost flinch. It hadn't crossed my mind that the two of them would be in contact. *Of course they'd talk to each other. Who wouldn't after what happened? And they both care about you.*

"We pulled a Nancy Drew on the files yesterday," I say, keen to change the topic.

Nerissa's eyes widen. "And?"

I fill her in.

"That's horrible," she exclaims. "They're just going to kill those three girls?"

"Not if we can get to them first." Now it's my turn to strum my fingers nervously. "Are you up for a road trip?"

She claps her hands. "Where to?"

"Mackay, Airlie Beach, and Townsville."

"I could definitely think of worse places to go. When?"

I want to demand now, but instead I go with,

"ASAP. We can't be certain, but Connor found an itinerary that hits all three spots at the beginning of next week. Even though it indicates they're not scheduled to be eliminated until next year."

"Dylan would probably have to come. Are you cool with that?" she asks. I go rigid at the thought of another person knowing my secret. She must have noticed as she then blurts out, "I haven't told him your secret, and I won't. All being well, we won't have to either."

The tension disintegrates from my body. "That's all good. I've already asked Ryder. That'll balance things and not raise suspicion from my parents."

"Good. Let's do some research." She clutches my hand and tugs me towards the house. "We need to check flights and somewhere to stay. I agree, the sooner the better. Next week would be great. I won't be too far into the uni term for it to matter."

We lapse into silence as we slip in the back door. Nerissa's parents sit at the kitchen table, coffee cups in front of them. They give us a little wave as we pass. Nerissa wiggles her fingers at them as though she's taking her best friend to her room for a gossip session instead of planning to save a group of girl's from a crazy man. I can't believe my luck that she came into my life when she did.

Nerissa grabs her laptop and gets in her zone, making lists and preparing our itinerary. I lay on her bed and prop my head on my hand, making suggestions where I can. She definitely wants to help and everything else she's said is genuine. A heavy weight rests on my heart that she doesn't trust me enough to tell me what's really going on, especially with what she knows about me. I want to confront her, but won't jeopardize the mission to save my sisters…or our friendship. After about half an hour the boredom of planning overtakes me and my eyelids get heavy. My blinks get longer until my eyes don't reopen and I rack out.

Ryder? Ryder where are you?   Fog against black. Nerissa? Anybody? Mist and darkness surround me.   I stumble forward. Please don't leave me, I'm sorry. My hands reach into the black, groping for anything. But there is nothing.

"Forget Ryder. He'll leave you, abandon you. Just like Colin and your mother." The voice snakes through my mind, hurting my head.

Confusion gnaws at me. Mum has never left. I clutch handfuls of hair as I curl into a ball, praying the voice will go away. The dreams feel worse when he is in them.

"Not her. Not the one pretending to be your mother. Your real mother." I recoil at his invasion of my inner thoughts. "You prayers won't save you. Give in now and come to me."

"No!" I run away from the voice, stumbling as I go. Then, the man with the long brown hair materializes before me.

"Run if you like, Mishca. I will always be able to catch you," he sniggers. "Always."

I wake with a shudder. Drool trickles from the corner of my mouth. I wipe it off with the back of my hand. The dreams no longer get to me now. I know they're just some propaganda programming. I won't let them beat me. I focus on the details of the man's face — he has to be Wirth — but the memory eludes me. It's all a blur.

"Are you okay?" Nerissa asks.

"Yeah, I'm fine." I attempt to smooth down my messy curls. "Are you sure your parents will be okay with this? I know they're over protective and all that."

Nerissa nods. "I'm going to pitch it as a birthday treat. They know Dylan will protect me." She grins wickedly, so unlike the angelic face that's her default setting. "I know Dylan will do about anything I ask."

"Even a north Queensland road trip?"

"Yep. But we'll only have to do a little bit of driving. We can fly direct to Mackay at the end of the week, drive to Townsville with a stop off at Airlie on the way, and then catch another direct flight home." Her typing is almost hypnotic as she lays out the plan. "We've got to hire a car for the drive and find a place to stay. Caravan parks seem to be the cheapest if we book a cabin or villa. But we'll need to leave booking the flight back until we're in Townsville since we have no idea how long it will take."

My dream flashes back through my mind. Icy fear fingers walk up my spine. What if my sisters are in immediate danger? "Let's go now, tonight. Just pack a car and go." My voice rises with each word. "We have to go now."

"Mishca," Nerissa says in a soothing tone, like she's talking to a crazy person. "We have a plan, an itinerary now. The wheels are in motion. If we race off with no idea of what we're actually doing, we could end up in trouble. And it'll raise suspicion from our families if we disappear tonight. We need this to be a believable holiday."

I inhale, willing my emotions to dial down. Pushing away the images of different dead and bleeding versions of me, I find a little Zen.

"So we're really going to do this," I ask, keeping the tremor that wants to overtake my voice at bay.

"As long as your parents aren't going to be an issue." Nerissa knows how over protective they can be, just like hers. "How are you going to tackle them?"

"I'm going to talk to them. I'm hoping they'll be in a receptive mood."

"Sounds like a plan. Well, part of a plan." She wrings her hands together. "Have you really thought this through? I mean I will totally be there for you. But I think there's some other things to consider."

The frustration and anger I've been bottling up since discovering I'm a clone threaten to boil over. I grit my teeth. "Like what?" The words are harsh.

"Like what are you going to tell your sisters when you rock up on their doorstep? And what are you going to do after that?" Nerissa sounds apologetic.

A horrible stone of despair rolls around my guts. I push it away. My hands find the pillow and I grip it tight like it will protect me from her doubt.

I can make it okay. I can rescue them.

"Even if you can convince them that they aren't safe, how are you going to protect all three of them?" Her probing question stabs at me. "Are we going to collect clones and end up with four of you together on a road trip, or on a plane together? Are you going to hide them at your place and tell your parents you all are quadruplets?"

The sound of ripping fabric is accompanied by bits of poly-fill floating in the air.

'You don't understand," I yell. "I have to rescue them. I'm the only one who can." I stare at the decimated pillow in my hand, ashamed at my outburst. She only wants to help.

"You're probably right. I'm just trying to help you think this through." She places a cool hand on my arm, sending small goosebumps rippling across my skin.

I take a deep breath. "Honestly, Nerissa, there's too many variables to tell where this is going to go. None of them may believe me, and then I'll be powerless to save them. But at least they will have been warned."

She smiles at me, a sad smile of pity. Her gaze weighs on me, compounding the heavy stone of bleakness that sits in my belly. We sit in silence for a few moments until she reaches over to her drawer and grips a present the size of a shoebox. It's wrapped in blue paper with penguins on it.

"Here. It was meant to be for your birthday, but I was hoping it would show you that we're still good — no matter what."

"You didn't have to." The douche-iness of my outburst brings on the shame. "I haven't even gotten you anything yet and your birthday is," I count in my head, "Thursday!"

My sad-sackness has really impacted on my usually

effective present shopping. I tear at the paper to reveal a pair of gorgeous blue sapphire earrings. I slip them in, clipping each one in place.

"That's okay. What kind of best friend would I be if I got angry at you for forgetting with everything that's going on?"

"You still think of me as your best friend?" I ask cautiously.

She beams at me, her whole face lighting up, and looks me in the eye. "Of course."

Truth! I hug her, forgetting to be gentle.

"Ouch, Mishca!"

"Whoops. Sorry."

Nerissa bites her lip and glances at me. "Do you really think you can save them?"

I shrug. "I don't know. But I have to try."

CHAPTER 2

RYDER

"HEY." EVERY PART OF ME lights up as Mishca answers the door, apple and fruit knife in hand. She is a mismatch in her black sequined dress, but somehow sexy. I have to remind myself we are only friends...for now.

"Come on in, I'm nearly ready."

I follow her into the kitchen, listening to the sharp crunch as the knife bites into the apple. Her munching fills the empty space between us. She is right there, within reach, but romantically I am back at square one and dare not touch her without a signal it is okay. No matter how much I want to.

She leans casually against the bench and slices into the last piece of apple to remove the seeds, staring peculiarly at the fruit knife. Smelly Belly, her Himalayan Persian cat, rubs against my legs on her way to Mishca. The furball flops onto her back at Mishca's feet, exposing her feline underbelly in a demanding way. Mishca absentmindedly obliges, rubbing her foot over the fluffy tummy.

Oh to be that cat.

"Ryder!" Mrs. Richardson pops her head around the corner. "I thought I heard you. Could you help me for a moment? I need to move something and Tom's at a meeting."

"I could, Mrs. Richardson, but would I?"

Mishca groans. *Okay, that is getting old.* Mrs. Richardson does not seem to notice and beckons me to follow.

We make our way down to the garage. "So what do you need me to move?"

"Nothing." Mrs. Richardson purses her lips and taps her chin. I brace myself for the onslaught of parental protectiveness. "Ryder, I'm really worried about Mishca. She hardly eats. She doesn't seem to sleep. The other day I caught her with my sleeping pills—"

"Well, if she is not sleeping."

Mrs. Richardson rolls her eyes. "Please keep a close watch on her." I nod and turn to walk away when she catches my wrist. "And Ryder, if you ever hurt her I will personally cut your balls off and feed them to you on a platter."

That is an image that I really do not need.

I nod, pad back upstairs, and pause at the kitchen doorway to watch Mishca as she gazes intently at her hands. She is so beautiful, but so sad. The fruit knife blade glints in the light as she raises it to her wrist and pulls it across the skin.

"Mishca! No!" I race to her side and seize her arm to

compress the wound. No blood oozes between my fingers or appears anywhere in sight. I stare into her confused brown eyes until she crumbles into my chest, sobbing.

"I'm so sorry." The knife clatters on the tiled floor.

"Shhh, hush now." I stroke her hair gently. "It is going to be fine."

"I-I wished I had n-never b-been m-made."

I pull from our embrace, but still hold onto Mishca's shoulders. "Do *not* ever say that."

Mishca struggles from my grasp and takes a few steps away. "I can't do it anyway. I can't even bring myself to cut hard enough to break the skin. I couldn't bring myself to take Mum's sleeping pills either. I'm too scared. I don't want to go to hell. I just want to evaporate."

I pick the knife off the floor and place it on the side of the sink. "It will be okay. You will see. You need to give it some time." My hand reaches for her again, even though it feels like an invasion of space. The tension in her body seems to fall to the floor as she lets me hug her. Some warmth stirs inside me and I wish I could hold her forever. Then, I remember Colin and I resist the urge to clench my fists.

"I want it to be how it was before — when I used to be normal; when I was just me, not a..." Mishca rests her forehead against my chest, "a freak."

"You do remember I am the one that glows and levitates?" I tap her lightly on the shoulder. Mishca nods, amusement tugging at the side of her mouth. "If anyone is freakish here, it is me. I go blue. We may be different, but we can be different together." I gulp at the sound of the truth. I miss being with her so much. "I do not think we are alone in this world. People may seem normal on the outside, but beneath the surface..." I trail off as the memory of me comparing her to a deep river invades my mind. Back when we were together.

She stays quiet as if contemplating my words.

"Really nothing has changed except your knowledge on the situation, and your perception of yourself. You have always been," I pause slightly before uttering the word she hates, "a clone. You were for more than eighteen years of your life without any negative impact—"

Mishca pushes away from me and raises an eyebrow.

I correct my error. "With minimal impact on your life."

Both eyebrows go up.

Yes, her heart defect was due to her original's health problem, but she was missing the point.

She does not seem to notice my lack of words. "I need a minute."

I fold my arms, tucking my hands securely under my biceps, and resisting the impulse to envelop her in my arms. After a moment I ask, "Do you want to stay in tonight?"

"No, I think a good night out will help me get back to normality. Besides, we need to meet up with the others and finish our strategizing and maybe I can do a patrol and some recon."

"Are you sure?" I am tempted to argue against her

plan, but do not want to put her back in a downward spiral.

She nods, but bites her bottom lip. "My sisters need me. I have to be strong until Friday at least. I think I will be okay once I'm on the mission."

I stiffen at her choice of words. Even her vocabulary is going military.

Abruptly she says, "Do you think maybe your mum is British? That could be the go with your lack of contractions?"

Mishca often goes off on tangents, but this one catches me by surprise. "My what?"

"Lack of contractions, come on grammar nerd." Mishca punches me lightly in the arm.

"Oh. That. I do not. Um, I do not know. I mean I don't know." My tongue wants to rebel, resisting the word. She has made fun of me for my speech before, but it always catches me off guard. "I have not noticed it with my parents. They are, they're British too. Let us– I mean let's check next time we are there." It almost hurt to let those words pass my lips. But I should make an effort to stop sounding so proper.

Mishca laughs. "It's not that big of a deal. It's one of your quirks that I love so much."

She said love. I want to kiss her so badly right now. "Come on, we'd better get going. Nerissa will be wondering where we are."

***

Last time I was at the Bowl, Mishca had been with Colin. I flinch at the memory. It had almost killed me that night to see her with him. But tonight, the world is as it should be, well almost. It would be better if Mishca's hand was entwined in mine.

We shift through the mass of gyrating bodies and head towards our private booth. In the middle crowd Sophitia's green mane flies around as she moves to the music. A smile creeps across my face. I have always had a connection to Sophitia, not in a romantic way, but more like kin. We clicked as buddies from the day we met.

Nerissa waves at us as we move towards her group. They could all pass for Swedish backpackers with their various shades of blond hair. Apparently, their families are tight, and Mishca confided in me that they are all betrothed to each other. Kind of odd, but to each to their own. Dougie and Nixie are the only ones not coupling up, apparently still on a break. At least that makes things a little less awkward for Mishca and me not being third wheels.

Nerine and Dorian scoot over to let Mischa and I squeeze into the booth. Warm hellos come from all around. I notice the empty glasses and offer to buy a round. "What is everyone having?"

"Anything but absinthe," the group choruses and the girls giggle. I feel out of the loop on that joke. I glance at Mischa to make sure she is okay. When she grins at me, I reciprocate and then head to the bar to order a couple of jugs. Sophitia's friend Coen is at the bar in a heated discussion with a young man.

"They are all accounted for, are they not?" Coen spits at the dark-haired young man. "I met him through Sophitia. How about you ask her, Adair?"

I met Coen through Sophitia! Are they talking about me? Adair turns to leave, causing his eyes to meet mine. His blue eyes narrow as he inspects me, then he stalks off. A strange aura came from him, almost like heat. I know I have felt something like that before, but cannot place where. Coen shrugs, a large grin plastered across his face that seems to stretch his mouth unnaturally. I get the distinct impression that I will not get a straight answer if I ask what that was about, so I decide not to bother.

I return to the tables with a pitcher of some cocktail the girl behind the bar recommended as well as a pitcher of beer. Mishca whispers to Nerissa and appears much more like her old self. Maybe she was right; maybe this is what she needs.

Applause erupts as I get closer — apparently the girl behind the bar gave me good advice. The girls all take a deep drink after calling, "Cheers" and clinking glasses. Mishca sips hers delicately, seeming very much like she is still getting used to the concept that she can now drink alcohol. Eventually, she leaves her glass on the table, only half consumed.

"Let's dance!" Mishca cries as a new song blares from the speakers and fills the club with a pulsating beat. Her cool hand slips into mine as she tugs me from my seat. I give no protest. Being close to her without having her as mine is painful, but not as bad as watching her in the arms of another. We weave through the mash of flailing arms until we find a small space on the dance floor where we can move.

I love watching Mishca dance. She closes her eyes

and brings her hands above her head as though she is basking in the melodic sounds — if you can call this type of music melodic. She sways in time to the beat, unaware of my gaze fixed on her. Her smooth caramel skin glistens in the strobe lights and her hair spirals as she moves.

My hands itch to touch her hips, but I leave the gap between us. Involuntarily, I glance over at the dark corner where we made out early in our relationship, the night of her show-and-tell striptease. My mouth twitches.

It does not take long for sweat to trickle down our necks. Mishca's brown eyes stare at me as intently as mine had earlier. My heart skips a beat and then pulses with the bass. She clutches at my arms and pulls me closer, locking our hips together as we move to the music. It takes all my self-control not to taste her lips.

The first time I kissed her was here on this dance floor. We moved to the beat as one, like we are now. Maybe she is thinking the same thing too. Maybe we can start things up again. The way she gazes at me, like she is kindling waiting for a lit match to touch her, waiting to be ignited. It burns me up inside.

Mishca leans in, her breath hot on my ear. "I need to go to the loo." I laugh inwardly, not the romantic interlude I was hoping for. I nod and withdraw from the dance floor with her, holding her hand until the last possible moment as she retreats to the ladies.

I push through the throng of revellers towards our booth and then stop in my tracks. Dread ripples over me. Something evil is here. A guy shoulders into me and forces me to take a step back. He turns, glaring with dark eyes behind long brown hair. A heat emanates from him that causes my eyebrows to pinch together in concentration. A knot tightens in my stomach.

"Hey-" As I reach for him to demand an explanation, he shimmers and glides from my grasp.

"Another time, *boy*." With that, he disappears into the crowd. I glance around, frantically wondering why I can feel his presence as I had Adair's. Yet Adair's was nowhere near as potent as this guy's. It dawns on me that I have felt them both before — at Mishca's! Last year when I was dropping her home, I sensed them near her house. It creeped me out then, just as it has now.

Oh, shit, Mishca! What if he is here for her? What if that was Wirth?

I shove people aside as I barge towards the toilets. *She is okay; she will be fine.* I reassure myself, but the sinking feeling in my stomach persists.

I am sure that was Wirth and he is here to claim Mishca.

CHAPTER 3

MISHCA

"HEY! WHAT DO YOU THINK you're doing?" cries a girl in front of my cubicle. Someone starts to speak, but is cut off by more girls screeching in protest.

I twist the lock across and peek through the crack. *What the — ?*

"This is the girls' toilet, mate." A brunette girl whacks Ryder with her clutch.

"I just wanted to —"

"Ryder?" I push free. "What are you doing?"

His fists unclench. "I thought you were in danger."

The brunette gives us the stink eye and stomps from the restroom. I go over to the sink and wash my hands. I should never have let him see me with the knife. This level of over-protectiveness is ridiculous.

"Why would you think that?" I turn the tap off and flick my hands towards the basin, letting the water droplets splat against the porcelain.

"There was this guy with long brown hair and he felt," he pauses and purses his lips as if searching for the word, "evil. Though I have never seen him before, I sensed him at your place. I think he is Wirth."

I tense up. "You felt him at my place? And he had long brown hair?"

Ryder nods.

"That sounds like the guy from my dreams. You're right, it could be Wirth!" I snatch at Ryder and yank him behind me as I rush from the restroom. "Where?" I demand, not wanting to miss the opportunity for some answers, and at the possibility of giving this guy an ass-whooping. The pain he's caused me, and the pain he's going to inflict on my sisters, more than warrants it.

I can't believe how easily I can call them my sisters.

"Ouch, Mishca. I need this arm," he says with a pinch of frustration in his voice. I let loose my grip as he surveys the club. "I cannot see him."

"The cameras," I gesture to the surveillance glass domes set in the ceiling, "The club has to have them."

I march over to Nerissa, ignoring her Dylan-snuggling. "I need to see the security cameras."

"What?" She pulls away from her fiancé and stares up at me.

"Your uncle's security cameras. My, ah," I almost say maker, "stalker. He was here."

Her face goes pale.

"You've got a stalker?" pipes in Dorian, concern passing over his face.

"I don't think we'll be able to get them tonight. But I'll ask." Her face screws up in uncertainty, but she's not lying to me. I've been watching her more carefully since the incident at her house.

"Now." It's a demand, not a request.

Nerissa squeezes from the booth and leads me to a backroom, Ryder close behind. Inside, her uncle sits at a desk, talking on the phone. When he doesn't immediately get off the call I snatch the mobile from his hand and press the end button, resisting the urge to hurl it across the room.

"Mishca!" Nerissa's shrill voice pierces through the haze clouding my mind.

"Sorry." I turn to her uncle. "I am so sorry. It's an emergency."

"Lucky for you that call wasn't important. And any friend of Nerissa's..." He leers at me and my skin crawls. Though I'm glad it fades when he sees Ryder.

"There's a guy here with long brown hair. He's been stalking me, but I've got no proof. I need to see the security footage so I have evidence." The lie rolls off my tongue way too easily.

He nods and moves to the wall, sliding back a false panel I hadn't noticed to reveal screens. My situational awareness totally failed me. *How did I miss that? Come on super-soldier senses, you're letting me down.*

"How long ago?"

I estimate the time and he rewinds it. I scan the screens and spot the reversing image of Ryder at the girls' toilets.

"This one," I point to it, "A bit further back."

When it gets to Ryder standing still at the edge of the dance floor I ask him to stop and play it forward. The long hair is hauntingly familiar. Then he turns his face towards the camera, his eyes glinting red. It's him.

It's Wirth.

Revulsion shudders through me.

Nerissa's uncle tracks Wirth's movements in the club to the point where he leaves. The two of them murmur things to each other that I don't bother listening to at all. Thoughts battle each other like a full on melee where everyone's ass is getting kicked.

"Do you want me to send this to the police?"

I shake my head, realizing there is nothing I can do with the video. Nowhere to report him. No one to help me. But now, I know my dreams weren't lying about him. He's real.

"I'll give his image to security."

"Okay, thanks for your help, Uncle Conway." Nerissa pushes me through the door.

I head across the club like a zombie with no fresh meat in sight. The conversation floats around me. I ignore the words, concentrating instead on the stranger in my dreams and imagining my fist connecting with his face.

Nerissa whispers something to me, jerking me back to the here and now.

"What was that?" I swivel to face her.

"My parents said yes and Dylan loves the idea of a getaway week for the university break," Nerissa whispers. "I haven't told him about your sisters. Do you want me to?"

"Negative. Hopefully, I can warn them without drawing attention to us. He doesn't need to know."

Any chance of feeling normal disappeared the moment Wirth decided to show himself to Ryder. The night has officially tanked. I glance at Ryder, hoping he can tell that I want to leave. I incline my head towards the door. He nods and gets up.

"We're out." I snatch up my jacket and clutch.

"Sure thing." Nerissa hugs me. "We'll talk tomorrow?"

"Don't do anything I wouldn't do," calls Douglas with a smirk. "Which means nothing is off limits."

I raise an eyebrow as Douglas winks. Romance is the last thing on my mind. It was fun dancing with Ryder, but I'm not ready — even if he is. It's so hard when my feelings for him are still there and strong, but the residue of Imogene's love for Colin stains my heart. I'm her replica. My love for Colin was a duplicated feeling run through a photocopier way too many times. I need to sort my counterfeit feelings from my real ones. I can only have faith that Ryder still wants me when the shit storm is over.

Everything is so confusing right now. So I resist the urge to hold his hand again as we leave the club. The last thing I want to do is lead him on, even though I may have already done that on the dance floor. My body took over on instinct there. If he'd led me to our secluded corner to reminisce about our make-out session, I would've let him.

I groan as I step onto the street. My head hurts thinking about it.

"Are you all right?" Ryder asks.

"Yeah. A little tired. I may have tried too much too soon." I put on a happy face with my feeble response. I jam my hands into my pockets so they stay unclasped.

It'd be too easy for Ryder to touch his fingertips to mine.

"Are Nerissa and Dylan all set?" Ryder asks as we head to the car park.

"They're good to go. I've just got to tell my parents." I grimace. "Even though I'm technically an adult, I still can't help feeling like I need their permission. You know, living under their roof and all. Stupid, huh?"

The sides of Ryder's mouth quirks up. "Not at all. I get it. It took a while to find out who I wanted to be instead of allowing my parents to determine my life choices. My gap year helped. Maybe yours will too."

I manage to return a grin before sliding into the car.

The ride home is murder. I want nothing more than to be in someone's arms—Ryder's arms—and to heal. But there's no time for those shenanigans; my sisters need me. I have to focus, not allow distractions. I sit rigid in silence the whole way home, lost in the realization that I was in the same building as my creator, the man who wants to kill the other versions of me.

A prolonged stillness in the car brings me back to reality.

Ryder grins at me and my heart wants to break for not kissing him this instant. "Lost in thought?"

"I was thinking of my sisters."

"Good," he says. "Think of them. They need you."

I sense subtle undertones. "It's okay. I've managed to keep those thoughts at bay."

I leave the car and Ryder follows.

"You don't have to walk me to the door. This isn't a date." It comes out harsher than I intend.

He pulls a face complete with wounded puppy eyes. "Thanks for the reminder. I still want to make sure you get home safely. Your mother made threats to my manhood."

I laugh, not being able to picture my mum getting the upper hand physically on anyone, and we head to the door.

"Okay, well, we'll talk tomorrow. I'll let you know how it goes with my parents."

Ryder makes no move to leave, his gaze roaming between my eyes and lips. My resolve wavers. He leans closer and I do too.

"Hey, Ryder. Want to come in for a coffee," Dad says as he opens the door.

We jump apart and I find myself disappointed. *Where did that come from? Now is not the time.* I wrinkle my nose at Dad's lack of tact. It's not like I'm sixteen. To his credit, Ryder gives Dad a warm response and comes inside.

"Really, Dad?"

He gives me the most innocent expression, but his eyes sparkle with mischief. Mine do a clockwise spin simultaneously.

"Hello," Mum calls from the kitchen. "Tom, why don't you and Ryder take a seat in the lounge room while Mishca and I get the drinks ready?"

Ryder dutifully follows Dad, leaving Mum and I alone in the kitchen. Now is the perfect time to ask Mum about the road trip, minus Dad. Divide and conquer ninja skills.

"So, Mum." I make sure to speak very slowly and deliberately.

"Yes, honey," she answers, putting some leftovers away.

"I was thinking it might be nice to go up north. You know, for a bit of fun seeing as I didn't get to go to Bali last year." I endeavor to gauge her reaction and guilt trip her. Can't hurt.

Mum picks up cups and the coffee. "Oh, that sounds like fun. Where should we go? Cairns?"

I bite my lip, and then plunge in. "Actually, I was thinking that it would be me, Nerissa, Dylan, and Ryder going for Nerissa's birthday."

Mum spins to face me, but her gaze goes to the doorway over my shoulder.

"And you four would be going where?" The voice belongs to my dad.

I may be charged up with super-soldier powers but I still need to work on my ninja skills apparently.

My mouth becomes absent of saliva as I search for an answer. I gulp in an effort to get enough moisture so I can form words. "To Mackay and Airlie Beach and then Townsville for a road trip so we can have some fun before the others get back fully into their studies."

Dad folds his arms. *We're boned.* "Are Nerissa's parents okay with this?"

"She checked with them and they're cool with it. It was actually her idea. She thought it would help me get over the thing with my birthparents." My voice trails off as I nearly choke on the words.

"And you would have separate rooms?"

"Yes." *One for me and Ryder, and one for Nerissa and Dylan most likely. But separate beds for Ryder and me.*

"And when would you be going?"

"End of the week and we'll be back for her winter term of uni. She arranged everything." Which is true, kind of. Her uni will have already begun by the time we get back, but she won't miss much. And she did the itinerary while I drooled and dreamed.

I bite on my lip as Dad takes the longest pause.

"Sounds like fun. How about we chip in for some spending money?" My heart skips a beat. I jump up and down on the spot, and then hug Dad. I lost my job at the ice creamery after my meltdown and, thankfully, my parents took pity on me financially so far.

"You can't be serious, Tom?" Mum exclaims.

"She is an adult, Alicia. We can't actually stop her. And she's missed out on so much. But now she's better. It's time for her to live her life to the fullest. Besides, her and Ryder are only friends now." Dad's gaze shifts from me to Ryder pointedly, and then back at me. "You dodged a bullet with your heart transplant, don't do anything to put yourself in harm's way, you understand?"

I nod so hard that I end up doing a bobble head impersonation. Mum sighs, but throws her hands in the air. *Yes! Surrender.*

"Come on." Dad cradles his cup in his hands. "Let's enjoy this coffee."

We sit in the living room, Mum and Dad in their chairs with Ryder and I on the lounge, but there's a distance between us that's more than just air.

"How's university going, Ryder?" Dad asks.

I knew he wouldn't be able to resist.

"Great. My course is going really well. I am looking forward to next term."

"There's still time for you to enroll for next term?" Dad stares at me, eyebrow raised.

"No, applications ceased in June. But it's for the best. I need this year off." And time away from Colin. I could go to another university, but any classroom is likely to evoke memories I want to bury deep.

Mum comes to my aid, turning the conversation towards the latest scandal plaguing rugby league. My parents launch into a debate on whether one of my dad's players would be silly enough to get themselves into trouble with the police.

"They said yes," I whisper to Ryder.

All emotion drains from his face, leaving a neutral mask. "Are you sure this is what you want to do?"

"I have to try." I attempt not to plead or think about the new secrets I've hidden from him.

He puts on a happy face and something stirs inside me watching his face light up, something that I've been denying. "So be it, as long as we do it together."

His infectious optimism takes over me and I wonder why I'm resisting him. "I wouldn't have it any other way."

We stroll to the pool deck. The back half of it is in shadows as the new moon deprives that side of light. I stare at the potted plants at the far edge of the deck, remembering when I hurled one over the edge in frustration.

Threat detected.

I place a hand on Ryder and freeze. At the back, in the gloom, stands a tall figure, cloaked in darkness that seems to be more than just the night. Light from inside the house should be throwing some on him, but it's not.

"What is it?" Ryder whispers.

"Can't you see him?" I whisper back.

The guy is huge. I'm assuming it's a guy because I've never seen a woman pushing seven-feet tall. He shifts forward for a moment and whatever was concealing him falls away, revealing the grey-skinned man who "helped" us escape from the warehouse and then promptly knocked us all unconscious.

Ryder stiffens. "You bastard," he says under his breath and goes to step towards the man-mountain.

I grip him tighter, keeping him in place. He winces, but my hand stays firm. Dressed in his now signature trench coat, the large man gives an acknowledging salute before vaulting over the rail. I sprint towards it with Ryder close behind. There is nothing but the usual dimness and shadows by the time I get to the edge, no matter how hard I look. I strain to listen and to pinpoint a location. No way a guy that size should be that swift. I hear nothing outside of the regular noise that surrounds us, except for the beating of wings.

CHAPTER 4

RYDER

I ENDEAVOR TO CONCENTRATE on everything that Connor says, but my thoughts keep slipping to Mishca. She stares at the bookshelf with a weird expression on her face as though she is contemplating the expanses of the universe.

"I've created hard and soft copies for you with all the information I could extract on your, ah, sisters from the eefers files." Connor scans through the files on his computer screen, appearing to have no clue how disengaged Mishca is from his words.

"Thank you. I am sure this will make things easier," I say as his gaze flicks to Mishca and then back at his laptop screen. Each time he peeks at her it is like he cannot decide if he wants to study her or run away from her as fast as his bony legs will carry him.

"Sure thing. Is there anything else you need?" Connor asks, sliding a USB stick into my laptop and downloading the files.

"Mishca?" I ask in an attempt to draw her into the

conversation. She glances at me for the first time in ten minutes. "Connor has given us everything he could on your sisters. Is there anything else you want before we go, like information on Wirth?"

She has a picture frame in her hand. "That can wait. The termination of my sisters is the biggest threat. Connor can work on that while we're gone and debrief us on our return."

"Knowing more on Wirth may be useful —"

"No." She places the picture back on the bookshelf. The face of Fin's father stares back at me from behind the glass. "It'll waste time. He isn't going to do this personally and we are ahead of them at this stage. Who knows how long it'll take Connor to decode the remaining files. We have what we need for now. We'll rescue my sisters and then plan a strategy for how we deal with Wirth after."

Connor nods. "I'll work on it while you're away."

"Thank you. I really appreciate everything you've done for me, even though you didn't have to." Mishca sounds like her old self.

"No problem. I've got to bounce. Call me if you need any remote IT support during your trip." He pushes the chair, scraping it in a screech that makes me wince.

"I'll get Ryder to contact you if we need more assistance from you on the mission." Her arm twitches. I half expect her to salute and dismiss him.

"Ah, sure thing." His face stays neutral, but his eyes dart to me in a way that makes it clear we need to talk, minus Mishca. He scoops up his stuff.

"Mishca, how about you look over the information Connor has given us and I walk him out?"

"Sure. There may be some intel I've missed." She sits rigidly in the chair and opens the first folder. Her gaze remains fixed on the pages as Connor and I make our exit.

As soon as we are hidden from Mishca's line of sight, Connor pulls his phone free and taps away on the screen. Then, a message pings on my phone. I reach into my pocket and see it is from Connor.

Don't talk. She can hear us if she wants to. Her programming is moving to a new level. She's switching between modes and could become unstable. Watch yourself with her.

I nod in reply and then delete the message from my phone, ignoring the hurricane of trepidation tearing me up inside. Mishca has to be okay. If only she would let me in, I am sure I could help her stay connected with her humanity.

"Later, man. Enjoy the trip, as best you can anyway."

"Sure thing. I will call if we need anything."

Connor retreats to his car, casting me one last look before opening the door. I give him a short wave to show him I am not worried, even though I am. Not for my safety, but for Mishca's sanity. How much can one person take before they reach that tipping point between coping and being ready to jump into the abyss? I know she wants it to end. *I will not let that happen.* I trudge along the front lawn and back inside, considering Connor's message. Is there something he has seen on the files that I missed about her programming?

Mishca still sits at attention in the chair, but staring at the bookshelf again, not the files.

"Will he be coming back?" she asks, her gaze unmoving.

"No," I reply. "But if you need to see Connor again before we go, I can arrange it."

"Not Connor," she gestures to the empty space on the bookshelf where the picture of my best friend's dad had been and then turns to me, "Finlay."

"I do not know." I squish my emotions into a ball of nothing. Finn's departure left a void right next to the loss of Mishca's love. Two holes to fill. And she feels bad enough about it.

"You shouldn't shun him because of me. You two have been friends for so long. I never meant to come between your friendship." Her voice sounds hollow and her face stays neutral, but her eyes fill with a sadness that would bring even the most cold-hearted bastard to his knees.

I resist the urge to rush over and hold her, but know my touch is no longer welcome that way. *Give her time.*

"He is being pig-headed." I sit down across from her, her hand inches from mine on the table. I want to tell her that he will come around, that our friendship can get past this, but the lie will not pass my lips. Instead I go with, "He knows where I am when he decides to stop being a dick."

"But if you stayed out of this, and told him you're sorry, then the two of you could be friends again." Her body relaxes and the military undertones disappear.

"But I am not sorry. No matter how many times or how many ways this could have gone down, I would always choose you."

Her lips twitch. I cannot tell if it is in happiness or dismay. My pocket vibrates before I can decide. I start to reach for it, but stop.

"It's ok. I'm not so fragile that you can't take a phone call." Mishca cocks an eyebrow.

I glance at the screen as Sherry's photo beams back at me. I go for the answer button so quick that I almost hit hang-up instead.

"Ryder, are you sitting down?" Her voice cascades over the line like an avalanche.

My head bobs affirmative. "Hit me."

"We've found her. And she's agreed to meet you."

Sherry says some more stuff, but I take little notice. *I am going to meet my mother.* Excitement and nervousness battle in my stomach like a pair of rock 'em sock 'em robots. I have wanted this for so long. What if it all goes wrong like it did for Mishca? I do not know if I am strong enough to handle what she went through.

"Are you still there, Ryder?"

I manage to find my voice. "Yes, I am here."

"Are you okay to meet her this Friday?"

"Sure." I scribble down the address and time on autopilot. Even though we leave Friday night, there is no way I will miss the chance to meet her...my mother.

When I put down the phone to talk to Mishca, she is nowhere to be seen. I shoot up and rush through the front door calling her name. *Stupid. So caught up in yourself, you did not even notice she was gone.* I make my way to the backyard. Mishca lays in the hammock, lazily scratching Jellyroll's belly as his tongue lolls across his lips in contentment. Her face is alight with joy, her mouth in a wide grin and rosiness spreads across her cheeks. It is tempting to stand and watch her forever.

"You scared me." I let my heartbeat slow from a staccato to a steady rhythm.

Her mouth straightens. "I know. I needed to do a perimeter sweep. I didn't want the enemy knowing about your mum. They could use that against us."

How can one statement be so accurate, and yet come across as so unhinged?

I go over the phone conversation in my head. I never mentioned my mother once. "You knew Sherry was calling about my mother?"

Mishca puts her index fingers behind her ears and waggles them at me. "Super hearing remember. I blocked it when I came outside so I could focus on any threats. When are we meeting her?"

"We?" I wince as soon as the word blurts forth. Inviting Mishca had crossed my mind, but I wanted to avoid the painful reminder for her that she would not have this reunion.

She sits up in the hammock, her eyes wide. "You don't want me there? I thought you could use some moral support, like how you've been there for me."

I stretch a hand to her and help her from the hammock. "I would love to have you there."

The cloudiness dissipates from her eyes, replaced with the sparkle I love. Relief floods over me. I was worried Connor was right about her mental state and that she wanted to be there to provide backup.

"It's settled then. Friday, you, me, and your birth mum." Mishca pulls her hand away from mine and sweeps some strays strands behind her ear. "Two birds with one stone. I get to meet your mum and can be there as backup."

CHAPTER 5

MISHCA

THE SILVER STARS ON THE blue wrapping paper glint in the sunlight. I flex my fingers against it, a little concerned at Nerissa's reaction. The box takes up most of my lap. Re-gifting isn't everyone's thing, but given the short timeframe I had, there wasn't much choice. I still bought her something too.

"You are not going to tell me what you got her?" Ryder asks, glancing at me before returning his focus to the road. "I can keep secrets."

"I know." The truth is I want to see his face as well. While I think the gift is both practical and thoughtful, everyone else might take it as my super soldier programming dominating me. And a little bit of me worries that I am no longer myself.

I squirm in my seat. Being so close to Ryder cuts inside like Freddy Krueger having a dance party. Every inch of me wants to be with him again. But it's so complicated right now. And then there's the whole issue with Sophitia being his cousin. The betrayal of not telling him sits in my stomach like I've eaten lead grapes. And that doesn't mix with the garden finger shears rave.

"Ryder." His name slides from my mouth before I even make the conscious decision to confess. But I can't have him leave with me tomorrow and not tell him this. "I have to tell you something, but I'm so freaked you'll be mad."

My somber tone hits the mark. Ryder pulls the car to the side of the road. "You can tell me anything. I will understand."

"This is different." My voices cracks. I gaze out the window to avoid those blue eyes. "I've kept something from you."

His warm hand finds mine. "After everything I know about you, do you really think I can be scared off?"

I swivel in my seat so I'm facing him. His face glows with adoration. I don't want that to disappear. Fear ripples across my skin knowing it will once he hears this. "It's not about me. It's about you."

He straightens but keeps his hand in place. "Go on."

I sigh, wanting to stare at the car floor, but knowing I need to see his reaction. "Sophitia isn't just your friend. She told me she's your cousin."

His face freezes.

Rambling takes over. "It was when we weren't together and she swore me to secrecy, and it probably doesn't even matter now because you're meeting your mum on Friday, but I had to tell you because it's been eating me up inside." I inhale deeply to compensate for the breath sapped away by the long verbal vomit.

"You should have told me." His trademark smile is nowhere in sight.

I bite my lip and nod.

"But Sophitia should have told me too." His voice catches. He withdraws his hand, instead gripping the steering wheel.

The cool air mockingly invades the space left behind. I want to reach for him, but stay rigid, wishing that my chair would turn into a black hole and suck me in.

A faint blue glow emanates from his fingertips followed by crackling mini lightning bolts dancing across his skin.

"Ryder." My voice holds no emotion, the cold, calculated part of me taking control. "If you don't get your emotions in check, you're going to set off a fireworks display in here."

As though he didn't hear me, his whole body begins to glimmer.

Out of here soldier. This job requires a tender touch.

I unclip my seatbelt, lean over, and kiss him. Zaps, like hundreds of static electric shocks, tingle across my lips. I force myself not to jerk away. Ryder responds to my touch, kissing me back with such enthusiasm that I lose all reason. We pull apart for breath. Then, Ryder bursts into laughter.

"Okay, not the reaction I was hoping for."

"I am so sorry, but," he hoots with laughter, "your hair."

I collapse into my chair, flip down the visor, and gasp. My almost-afro is now a full-on afro as though someone has spent all day rubbing my head with balloons.

"This is all your fault." I playfully slap his arm and then pat down my wayward hair. My tactlessness makes me wince.

"Sophitia's deceptions are not your fault." Ryder's hand cups my chin and steers my face towards him. "Besides, you were going through some major stuff. I will not hold that against you," a devilish grin crosses his face, "unless it means I get more kisses, because then I can hold it against you forever."

I laugh, but inside I squirm like a worm on a hook. Physical contact was all I could think of to pull him from the brink of a potential lightning meltdown. I may have all these super soldier skills, but I don't think I'm invulnerable to the electricity Ryder could potentially generate and I have no intention of finding out. Yet…it also wasn't my objective to have him believe we are back on.

"Ryder, I—"

"Mishca there is no need. You are not ready," he gives me a chaste kiss on the cheek and then turns the ignition key. "But I am patient."

We settle into a comfortable silence for the rest of the drive with my phone on random providing the background music. When we arrive, Ryder opens the door and takes the present from me so I don't have to juggle its bulk as I exit the car. He doesn't give it back, but continues to hold it for me as we head to the house.

Dorian welcomes us in, this time with me knocking on the door instead of almost on his face. Nerine appears behind him, practically bouncing with excitement, her blond hair swishing around her shoulders. "Come on through, we're all in the back."

Like Dylan and Nerissa, these two seem committed, despite the family obligation to each other. Lots of people find love in different ways. *Love.* Colin flits through my mind and everything inside churns. I force my gaze to Ryder and I find the warmth and calm that comes over me reassuring. I do love Ryder. How long can I keep him at a distance because I'm afraid of who I am and what I may become?

We follow them through the house to the back. Ryder and I are obviously the odd ones. For starters, we're the only ones without blond hair. When I step onto the porch it's like every single pair of eyes are on me. I try to dispel any super soldier paranoia. Yet as I sweep my gaze across the group of five sets of parents and their offspring, everyone is definitely staring.

Nerissa breaks the spell as she clears her throat and heads towards me. I cringe for a moment, wondering if Nerissa's group are secretly Aryan supremacists because the color difference is obvious. But I don't think that's it. I've experienced occasional racism, and it was never like this.

"Mishca, Ryder, come meet my parents." Nerissa's words break the spell. People begin talking amongst themselves again, except for her parents who beam at me and beckon me over. "This is my dad." She gestures to the tall man who could pass for Chris Hemsworth's father and then relieves Ryder of the present, putting it on the table with the other gifts.

Ryder extends an arm. "Mr. Murray."

"Please, call me Adrian." Something weird passes between them, almost an alpha-male posturing. But it's something else. Like they're assessing each other; hands clench together in a shake that's gone on for way too long.

Mrs. Murray coughs. The two guys release their grip and take a step back. Nerissa mouths *Dad* to her father. He grins and shrugs while Ryder's eyes widen in bewilderment.

"And this is my mum."

"Nadia." Her mother beams at us, inclining her head in a brief nod. "Come, grab a drink and something to eat."

A seafood spread sits on a table off to the side of the pergola.

"Thank you." Something is off here, but I can't put my finger on it. I do my best to act like a normal teenage girl celebrating her friend's birthday and ignore the warning prickling at the base of my neck. "It all looks so delicious."

My mouth waters at the amazing smorgasbord, but every inch of me is on alert. No funky conversations come to the attention of my hearing, no matter how hard I strain to listen to everyone's conversations. Dylan and Nerissa's exchanges are so hot, my face flushes. If they're like that the whole time we're away I might go insane. Apart from some tension between Dougie and Nixie, everything is a normal gathering of friends.

I purse my lips. Scanning the perimeter, I curse inwardly for not having done a sweep as soon as we arrived. *Nothing.* I make an effort to settle into a pleasant conversation with Ryder, Dorian, and Nerine.

After dinner, I excuse myself to go to the bathroom. I let the cool water from the taps run over my hands and splash water on my face. Staring in the mirror, I tap the middle of my forehead. "Stop glitching. Can't you be normal for once in your life?"

I pat the hand towel across my cheeks and brow, take a deep breath, and then make my way back to the party, willing my normal side to take control.

A large multi-tier cake with thick white icing has appeared on the table and Nadia busies herself placing nineteen candles on it.

"Do you think you can blow all those out?" I whisper to Nerissa as I sneak up behind her.

She jolts in surprise and giggles. "I'll give it my best shot."

The candle lighting is perfect. The sun disappears behind the tree line, allowing nineteen perfect flames to dance above the cake. A happy rendition of "Happy Birthday" rings from the crowd as we all huddle behind my best friend. Her shoulders pull back when she inhales and then relax forward as she blows across each candle, snuffing the flames. Everyone applauds.

"That is some lung capacity you have." Ryder cocks an eyebrow.

"Lots of swimming will do that," Dylan says. He gives Nerissa a kiss on the cheek. "I think Nixie will burst if we don't get to the presents."

Mr. Murray plugs in some fairy lights. A soft glow settles over the party. Nerissa opens each present carefully, folding the wrapping paper and handing it to her mum. Books, jewellery, a stuffed seal from Dylan, and clothes. Then, she gets to my gift. I want her to rip at the paper to get to it quicker. She narrows her eyes at the plain brown box. Flipping open the flaps, she spies the bracelet with a small heart charm with *BFF* engraved on it. It's nothing like the earrings she gave me, but it's the best I could do on short notice.

"Oh Mishca. It's beautiful." She slips it on and hugs me. "Rather big box though for this."

"There's another present underneath." I grin.

Nerissa pushes her hand through the small foam packing pieces and pulls free the black rectangular device.

"What is it?" she asks, peering at the top of it, about to press buttons.

"Careful." I lunge towards her and pull it away from her face. "The instruction pack is at the bottom."

"What did Mishca get you?" Nixie flounces over, extending her hand.

Nerissa passes it to her and searches for the instructions.

"They're in here somewhere." I rifle around as well and then make a triumphant cry as my fingertips connect with the booklet.

Too late I hear the hum. Nixie is too far away to reach without exposing my abilities. I grimace as the wires shoot forth and latch onto Dougie's chest. He convulses with the zaps and thuds to the ground in spasms.

Ryder rushes to my side. "You got her a Taser?"

CHAPTER 6

RYDER

I WIPE MY SWEATY HANDS against my jeans.

"You ready?" Mishca asks, giving my arm a squeeze.

I nod, but my insides refuse to stay still. My turn today; Mishca's turn tomorrow.

"How long until you think Dougie will talk to me again?"

"He will get over it soon. At least it got him and Nixie back together. I think everyone else there loves you for that."

An inappropriate chuckle rattles my chest. I did enjoy watching Dougie go down. He had made it clear he was happy to date Mishca last year. But it was disturbing that Mishca gave Nerissa a Taser for her birthday. Connor's warning floats around in my head. I do not want to watch her slip away into some robotic fighting machine, yet I am helpless to stop it.

"This is the house." Mishca stops in front of a home that is like every other one in the subdivision. It is so non-descript you would have to know the number to find it.

She opens the gate and motions me to come through. Hand-in-hand we walk up the path. I have to remind my wayward heart that her touch is for moral support, nothing more. But I am patient.

I take a deep breath, reach up, and knock on the wooden door. Muffled footsteps get progressively louder. The door swings open and a middle-aged man answers.

"Hi. You must be Ryder." He extends his hand. "I'm Gary, Rosie's husband. Come on in."

The interior matches the outside, bland and beige. Watercolor paintings line the hallway.

Gary catches me gawking and gestures to the pictures. "She loves to paint."

I was terrible at art in school. The only things I could ever do well were images like the sketches for my tattoos. I let Mishca get in front of me and trail behind as they move through a doorway. Everything slows down, my steps, their words. Unable to decipher what they are saying, I nod. I enter the room and look to the chair where my mother should be and see a stranger staring back at me.

"Ryder, this is Rosie, your mother." Gary gestures towards the timid brunette.

My insides freeze up. She is not my mother. This small mousy woman in a floral print lounge chair is not the mother I remember cradling me as a child, begging me to change. Everything else matches—all the paperwork Sherry showed me. This is the woman who gave me up for adoption. But she is not my mother.

"I guess you've got a lot of questions," my would-be mother says.

"Would you like us to leave you two alone?" Mishca makes a move to rise from her seat.

Rosie looks terrified at the prospect.

"A little moral support might be required," I whisper.

Gary sits on the arm of his wife's chair while Mishca and I sit together on the lounge. There is no space between us this time. She grips my hand and gives it a not-so-gentle squeeze. I grimace. She flinches.

"I guess you want to know why." The words stumble from Rosie. "I mean, that's what I was told you'd want to know."

She does not speak like me. As much as I am working on the whole contractions thing, I expected my mother to not use them much either.

"I guess that would be a good place to begin."

Her bottom lip begins to tremble. Gary rubs his hand across her back.

"You were the perfect baby when we first got you home from the hospital." She gazes up at her husband. "Not Gary. My first husband, Robert."

I shift uncomfortably in my seat, unsure if I want to hear the story when I know that she is not the woman I remember.

"You fed and slept for the first three weeks. All our friends were so jealous of us with this newborn that was such a little angel. Then—" Her voice cracks and her hand flies to her mouth.

Mishca glances over at me, her brows furrowing together. I keep my face neutral even though my stomach zaps with anxiety.

"I'm sorry. I thought after all this time I'd be okay." Rosie wipes away the trickling tears.

"There was a home invasion." Gary places a hand on his wife's shoulder. "Robert was killed."

I should feel something at the news my dad was murdered, but everything inside is as dead as he is. And he is not my father, if this woman is not my mother.

Rosie takes a deep breath. "And you were never the same. You cried all the time and no matter how much I fed you, it never seemed enough. You were never satisfied. It was like you knew your family had been torn apart.

"It became too much, losing Robert and your need for my constant attention. I fell apart and I gave you up. I felt like I had to or I-I don't know what I would have done to myself, or to you."

A red rash creeps up her neck and she makes a strange gasping noise. Then tears fall down her face, dripping off the end of her chin. "I'm so sorry I couldn't be the mother you needed."

Gary squeezes her shoulder. "Are you going to be all right to go on?"

Rosie nods, but her eyes fill with fear.

"No, I can come back another time," I cut in, torn between wanting to embrace her to take away her pain and run from the room...from this imposter.

My supposed mother nods. I give her an awkward,

but obligated, hug goodbye.

"We can see ourselves out," Mishca says, taking my lead. She still shoots me a look.

I follow her, fighting competing urges to punch a hole in the wall of the pristine home or to ruin it by allowing my breakfast to revisit.

Mishca waits until we are in the car to speak. "What's going on? You were acting like you couldn't wait to leave. You've been wanting this for so long."

My brow furrows as I search for the right words. "She was not what I was expecting."

"Oh, poor you. Some of us will never even get the chance to meet our mothers, or even have proper mothers! I don't even know if Imogene is technically my mother or if it's the woman who gave birth to her. Either way, there's no happy family reunion for me." The bitterness in her words is a slap in the face. But I cannot blame her.

I stare at my sneakers. "I know."

She sighs. "I'm sorry. I must be PMSing or something. I can't even begin to imagine what that would be like for you."

"Mishca, she is not my mother."

Staring at me with sad eyes, she reaches for my hand. "Of course she can't take Martha's place —"

"No, that is not it. I told you when we first met that I remembered my birth mother. She was not the woman I remember." I keep her gaze.

"Oh." Mishca bites her lip and her brows pinch together. "But she wasn't lying."

I raise an eyebrow. "Human lie detector too?"

"Yep, the level of freak keeps on rising."

"Please, do not be like that. You know I do not care how you came into being." I cringe inwardly at her offence to my question. I never want to hurt her.

"Okay," Mishca replies. She takes a deep breath and then continues, "Her body language was all wrong for someone who was lying. I can't confirm that she is your birth mother, but she is the woman who gave you up for adoption."

CHAPTER 7

MISHCA

"HOW CAN THAT BE?" Ryder asks, gripping the steering wheel tight so that his knuckles go a whiter shade of pale.

"I don't know, but a year ago if you had have told me that Dolly wasn't the only clone in the world I would've told you to pull your head from the sci-fi book you're reading and come back to earth." I want to reach for him, but can't.

He sneaks a weak smile at me and then returns his concentration to the road.

"Are you sure you don't want to blow off work?" I ask, worried that Ryder's state of mind could slip even more than mine. He's been so focused on this for so long that it must be devastating for him.

"I will be fine." But his voice does nothing to convince me.

And he needs the money. I sigh.

I'm hesitant to leave the car when we arrive at my house. Now we're both in pain, two broken people unsure of where we fit in the world. *Except for with each other*. I suck my cheek at the thought. I know I could help him heal. He could help me heal. Maybe soon I will give in to these feelings once more. But not now. Not yet.

We both make our way to the boot of the car and get his bags so he can head straight here after work.

"Call me if you need to." I hug him.

He nods. "I will see you this afternoon for the flight." He gets back in the car and drives away. He doesn't even give me a backward glance. That worries me more than anything else. Ryder's been there for me, but now he's in trouble and he might throw the walls up. Maybe I shouldn't have let him leave, should have ran beside the car and not care who saw. Show him I'm there for him, even if I did keep Sophitia's secret from him for too long. Why is everything going to the crap house?

I trudge up the stairs, a suitcase in each hand, longing for a time that I never thought I would — the days before my heart transplant. Back then I was unaware of my freaky nature. Back then Ryder hadn't shown me he could levitate and glow. Back then I believed I was born, not created. It feels so long ago.

I place Ryder's baggage at the door waiting for Nerissa to pick us up.

Mum leans against the kitchen bench. "How did it go with Ryder and his mum?"

"Awkward," I say, knowing it's the complete truth.

"Not surprising." She grimaces.

We lapse into silence. I can sense she wants to say

more, but I pray she doesn't. I'll dig more of a hole with each lie I have to tell them. Mum puts the kettle on and soon the sound of water heating fills the silence.

"Mishca, honey, are you sure you want to take this trip? We could go to New Zealand, or Disneyland?"

I take a deep breath. "This is important to me, Mum. Besides, we're all ready to go. Everything is booked and paid for. I can't back out on Nerissa now. It's for her birthday." That's a lie. Another lie that sits heavy on me. This trip is my call. If I don't want to go, the others would understand.

Mum comes over and embraces me hard. She can squeeze tight for someone with a model's build. Not that it hurts, but I can feel the pressure.

"I worry about you." She leans back and taps the tip of my nose with her finger. "I'm your mother, that's my job."

"I thought your job was to look beautiful," I tease.

She pulls a face that she would never dare with a camera nearby, making me laugh and then pops a bowl of strawberries in front of me.

I pick at my food, wishing we were already at the airport. Our flight to Mackay isn't until tonight, but I'm itching to get to there as soon as possible. We've decided to begin by visiting Michelle in Mackay, because from what we can tell she's scheduled for termination first, and then we'll drive to Airlie Beach to see Andrea, and finally, Townsville for Tammy. I can't let *those people* kill her or the others. Not that I know who those people are. But I don't care. I will save them. I have to.

Nothing tastes good as I force down the fruit under Mum's watchful eye. The last thing I want is for her to chuck a spaz and think I won't be responsible with my health while I'm away. I know my heart is fine now. The operation accidently triggered the super soldier programing, which led me to the cloning lab. Ryder told me I interacted with some super computer while I was there, and it may have helped with the healing process. As much as I hate that my heart transplant initiated all this, if I didn't have that surgery, I'd be on death row with my other sisters.

Plodding upstairs, I resume packing, which is basically checking I've got everything I need. My bags were ready straight after Mum and Dad agreed to let me go. This is busy work.

After giving everything the once over, I pick up the file Connor put together for me about my sisters and reread as much as I can. I get so absorbed in it that I lose track of time until there's a knock on the door. Nerissa pokes her head into my room.

"Ready?" Her face contorts between nervousness and excitement, the latter I suspect being faked on my behalf.

"Yep," I slide the file into my carry-on. "All packed."

"Okay, we might as well get going. Dylan's still in the car with Dorian. Grab Ryder and let's go."

"Ryder!" I glance at my watch. Nerissa is a little early, but there's only about thirty minutes till we agreed to meet up. "Where is he?"

I pace up and down. My hands wave frantically as

panic rises in my throat.

Nerissa grips me by the arms and holds me still. "Has Ryder ever let you down?"

"No." The word is barely a whisper. Even when I destroyed his friendship with Finlay, he's still been there for me. Even when I left him because I was confused about my feelings for Colin. Even when he learned I was someone else's copy. Even when I told him I'd kept the truth about Sophitia from him. I don't deserve his friendship, let alone his love.

"So what makes you think he would start now? Come on, let's get your stuff into the car. He'll be here soon. Are these his?" Nerissa kicks the bags in the doorway.

"Yep."

Nerissa gives me a quick hug. "It's going to be okay."

People say that, but that doesn't mean it will be. Still, I want to believe her.

She releases me and tries to pick up Ryder's bags. Her arms strain under the weight.

"Here." I step forward. "Let me."

"It's okay. I can take them." Nerissa takes two tentative steps before dropping them on the ground.

I pick up the bags easily. They feel like they're filled with feathers to me. My anxiousness about the trip and Ryder's tardiness has my mouth dry and a small sweat breaking over my skin.

He'll be here.

I take deep breaths and wait for Nerissa to open the door, willing my flipping stomach to stop the gymnastics routine. Ryder leans against Dorian's car, chatting with him and Dylan. I freeze at first, not quite believing my eyes. Then I drop my load and hug him. "You're here."

"Where else would I be?"

"How much stuff do you have in this?" Dylan complains as he lifts the bag into the boot.

Once the luggage is stowed, I hug Mum and Dad goodbye.

"You have fun now." Mum gives my arms a squeeze.

Dad clasps Ryder's hand. I can see that he's gripping hard. "I'm trusting you to take care of her."

I maneuver between them. "That's fine, Dad. We know you're still the alpha male in this fam-family," I stutter thinking of Finlay's dad.

Just breathe.

"Enough hanging around." I usher Ryder to the car. "Time for us to get going."

We all pile in, but it's a tight fit. I wave to my parents as they stand on the lawn and watch us drive away.

I wring my hands, worrying what's to come. Excitement and dread battle in my mind. *What if she doesn't like me? What if she won't believe me?* I push the thoughts down and try to stay positive. Tonight we'll be in Mackay and tomorrow I'll meet Michelle, my sister, my fellow clone.

CHAPTER 8

RYDER

MISHCA'S FINGERS TAP ON the inside of the taxi door as we head towards the motel. Rows of palm trees and tropical plants lit with the soft glow of orange streetlights line the Mackay roads. It is a nice change from the high-rise buildings of Brisbane's city center.

"It's kind of quaint, isn't it?" Nerissa leans over her fiancé to get a better view.

"I bet there's some awesome beaches." Dylan's hand plays with her hair as it swishes against him.

I look away, wishing I was next to Mishca instead of stuck in the back with these two love birds.

"There are some great spots around. I could take you for a tour if you want," offers our gangly taxi driver.

"No, straight to the motel," Mishca replies for us all in a clipped voice.

My muscles tense, unsure if her abruptness is her being a spaz or military-Mishca taking over again.

"Not a problem," the driver says. "It's not far now."

"Thank you."

Too polite to be in soldier mode. Must be freaked. And who can blame her when she is less than twenty-four hours away from meeting her sister.

The taxi driver pulls up in front of a high-rise motel in the city. So much for the agreed plan of keeping a low profile as backpackers. I grimace at Nerissa.

"What?" She grins. "It's the only place I could get that would fit us all with side-by-side rooms."

We pile from the car. Mishca pays the driver with cash while the rest of us unload from the taxi. Probably not the most well thought out plan considering how much Nerissa is struggling with her luggage.

"Here, let me help," I offer.

"It's cool. I'll help her." Dylan relieves Nerissa of a bag and tucks it under his arm before picking his stuff back up.

None of us packed light as we have no idea how long it will take to convince each of Mishca's sisters that they are in danger. For that matter, we have no idea how to protect them from the coming threat, other than to warn them it exists. Maybe Mishca is not the only one with her soldier programming triggered and they can protect themselves. At least they can get prepared.

Mishca comes over to where we have unloaded the bags and picks up more than her share, knocking my offer to help, and leaving Nerissa with only her handbag and me with my own stuff.

"I'll get us checked in," Nerissa says with a grin as we juggle the bags through the doors.

My skin tingles when the lower temperature air inside surrounds me. Mishca stands back, staring intently at her phone. I move towards her.

"Are you okay?" I ask.

"Yeah." She looks up from her phone and flashes the screen towards me. "She's only a few blocks away. How am I going to sleep knowing how close she is? Maybe I should visit her tonight?"

"Do you think that is wise? Turning up at night?" I place my hand over her arm in an attempt to be reassuring.

She flinches at first, but soon resignation overtakes her face and she sighs. "I guess not."

Nerissa walks towards us, jingling a room key in her outstretched hand while Dylan follows behind lugging their bags. Mishca reaches forward and takes it.

"We're on the top floor," Nerissa squees, practically bouncing on the spot.

The elevator feels claustrophobic, especially when I know Dylan is the only one with no idea of the potential trouble we could encounter. Connor assured me there was nothing in the information he unlocked, but they were watching Mishca. I felt them at her house and at the club. The best case scenario is this guy Wirth and his minions do not react in time. But if they do...I do not even want to think about it.

A ping from the elevator door brings me back to reality. Our rooms are far down the hall.

"We're going to have an early night." A sly smirk spreads over Dylan's face as Nerissa slides the key into their lock. "See you in the morning."

"Is that okay?" Concern sweeps over Nerissa's face.

"We'll be fine," Mishca replies. "It's like Christmas. The sooner we get to sleep the sooner we, err, can explore the city tomorrow."

"And you can do that family thing," Dylan adds, pushing Nerrisa inside. "Goodnight!"

Mishca unlocks our door and we dump the bags inside. The room gives off an eerie golden glow from the streetlights. I flick the switch on the wall and the room brightens. The problem is immediately apparent. One room. One bed, two armchairs. Oh boy. Tonight will be torture if we share a bed. How can I be so close to her without touching her? It will be the ultimate test of my self-control. The floor or chair would be a better option. I groan inside.

"We must have their room." I take the key off Mishca, spin on my heels, and head straight back into the hall. My fist pounds on our neighboring door. After some shuffling noises inside, the sound of thumping feet comes towards the door and a shirtless Dylan appears.

"What?"

Not exactly the nicest greeting, but not surprising either. Although, I thought they would have wanted the queen bed instead of the twin bed situation that was meant for Mishca and me.

"I think we got your room," I say as Nerissa pokes her head around the door, her dress on but dishevelled.

"What's wrong?" she asks.

"There is only a queen-sized bed in our room. I

figured that meant we have yours by mistake."

"Nope," Dylan cuts in. "We've got a big bed too, and about to make use of it, so later."

"Dylan!" Nerissa slaps her fiancé across the chest. "I'll call the desk."

"No." I spin around to see Mishca standing behind me, arms folded, head leaning against the doorway. "It's only for one night. We'll make do," she says in a voice so bland I cannot read anything into it.

"Are you sure?" I ask, my eyebrows pinching together, not sure whether to be excited at the prospect of sharing the bed, or freaked because I might accidently use her as a blanket. Then again, if I tried she might break my fingers on reflex.

She nods. "It'll be fine."

"You heard the lady." Dylan pulls Nerissa inside, shutting their door with muffled goodnights following.

"I could sleep—"

"In the armchair? On the floor?" Mishca cocks an eyebrow. "Don't be silly. And don't even think of suggesting that head-to-toe crap. I'm not spending all night smelling your feet."

I follow her back into our room. Mishca pulls some stuff from her bag, heads to the bathroom, and closes the door. I strip down to my boxers, staring at the bed the whole time.

"Do you need a turn?" Mishca points her toothbrush at the door.

The desire to grab my toothbrush overrules my eyes, which stay firmly on my ex. Her outfit probably would not be considered sexy, cotton boxers and a long-sleeve pajama top, but she is smoking hot to me. Every inch of me aches to touch her.

"Are you okay?"

"I am fine." I manage to croak the words.

I go on autopilot and get ready for bed. Next thing I know I am standing in the doorway of the bathroom with fresh breath, being a creeper again staring at Mishca as she lies in the bed under a thin sheet. I walk over to the light switch and flick it off and then slide in beside her.

"Thanks for coming," she whispers.

"There is nowhere else I would rather be."

With soft orange ambiance from the streetlights spilling onto her face, a longing sparks in her eyes. But then she closes them so I follow her lead, letting my mind drift off as it prepares to shut down for sleep. But instead of going to sleepsville, I keep thinking of that time at Mishca's where I snuck into her room and we snuggled until her mum busted us. Better than it being her dad. It would be so easy to touch her. My skin burns with anticipation. But my hands stay still.

Sleep pulls at me, the foggy realm begging me to give in. And I do. My breath deepens, slow and steady, and I let all the sexy thoughts of Mishca sing to me like a hot lullaby. Hand trailing up her thigh, lips together, her reaching for me. My mind combats the thoughts like a UFC heavy weight. The last thing I want to do is let dreaming-me hit on Mishca in reality. Time to think unsexy thoughts, but none come. Instead Mishca's hands on me dominate every inch of my mind, so much so it feels like it is really happening.

"Ryder."

My eyes spring open. Mishca stares back. Her hands are on me, pulling me towards her. I let her guide me until our lips touch. Then, I close my eyes again, grateful my dream is now reality.

As she continues to kiss me, Mishca inches closer until there is no space between our bodies. She reaches down, grasps the elastic of my boxers, and yanks me even closer until we are flush against each other.

I pull back and take in air. "Are you sure about this? After everything you have been through, and are still going through, I could be a complication or a mistake. I do not want to be your regret."

"Ryder." I shiver inside at the sound of my name on her lips. "I miss you so much. You make me feel normal, human. There have been times where it's like my emotions are switching off, like I'm getting detached. But when I think of you and the love I have for you, that side of me lessens."

"Wait a minute." I manage to find my voice. "You love me?"

She nods. "I couldn't deny what I feel for you. The love was there, probably even when I was with Colin, but that whole freaky soul mate thing clouded my mind and my heart. Not anymore. I've fought it for long enough, and I'll have enough fighting to do dealing with my creator. I'm not going to battle my feelings for you too." She waves her hand in the air. "I surrender."

My mouth goes so wide my cheeks ache. "That is all I need to hear."

CHAPTER 9

MISHCA

"MORNING," I MURMUR as Ryder wakes me with kisses. Every press of his lips makes me feel more normal, more human, and less like a robotic soldier girl.

Ryder pulls back for a moment and then trails the tip of his tongue over my lips. My heart races at a million miles an hour. This guy has followed me on a crazy clone-finding mission up the east sector of Queensland. That's devotion.

"Oi, come on, you two." A banging on the door accompanies Dylan's rough tone, spoiling the moment.

"Be there in a minute," Ryder says with a note of humor in his voice. Normally, we have to wait for them.

The morning sun lights our motel and I'm buzzing with excitement. Even Dylan's sour mood won't ruin today.

"I could get used to having you as my human teddy bear," Ryder teases as I wiggle from his arms.

Human. It's the first time in days the word hasn't put my teeth on edge since I discovered the truth of my origins. I must be growing up.

Another banging at the door. Ryder's hands drop and we both quickly get changed. I feel his eyes on me the whole time. I resist the urge to stare back.

I slip on jeans, a V-neck top, and a light jacket. It's not as cold here even though it's winter. I've gotten over hiding my scar. I don't know why. I just woke up a couple of days ago and found I didn't care. It's the mark of a survivor. Why should I be ashamed of that? Reaching behind my head, I pull my hair into a small ponytail. For good measure, I put on a pair of oversized sunnies and shove on a large hat. With enough of my features obscured I shouldn't be mistaken for Michelle by anyone. The last thing I grab is my pills that I have to take with breakfast.

"About time." Dylan rubs at his stomach. "I'm starving."

Ryder and I stroll hand-in-hand, which ignites the biggest smirk across Nerissa's face and a raised eyebrow from Dylan. The four of us walk a couple of blocks towards the heart of the city to pick up a cheap breakfast. Need to compensate for the expensive room somehow. We duck into Subway, order, and chow down.

After Dylan goes to the soda machine for a refill, Nerissa leans forward and speaks in a low tone. "Are you sure you want to go there alone?" she asks before taking another bite of her sandwich.

I nod. "It's going to be bad enough for Michelle to

have a doppelganger rock up on her doorstep without having an audience." I pick up my phone and open Maps to double check Michelle's address. "Besides, I can walk from here and then meet you at the shopping center. There's a water park you can visit."

"That sounds like a plan." Ryder shakes his shirt as though it will get rid of the humidity.

"The shopping part especially." Nerissa's eyes twinkle.

Dylan snorts when he re-joins us. "We're in paradise and you want to go shopping?"

Nerissa shrugs. "It's fun. Besides, Mishca has a lead to follow up on her birth parents." She's definitely better at lying to Dylan than she is to me. There were barely any signals.

We wolf down the rest of our food in silence.

"Do you think it's too early?" My nails find their way into my mouth as we walk outside.

"Everything will be fine." Ryder reaches for me, his hand creeping up around the back of my neck, and kisses me full on the lips. It's almost enough to make me want to go up to the motel room. Instead I pull away smiling and then turn in the opposite direction of the group. This is something that has to be done.

"Good luck," Nerissa calls as we part ways.

My insides twist when I follow the path to the Coopers' house. The first few blocks are full of retail stores and car yards. I rehearse what I'll say to Michelle. It's hard enough to tell someone they've suddenly got a long lost sister without adding insult to injury by going all Sci-Fi Mafia on them. *So you're a clone that someone wants dead.* Does she even know that she's adopted?

I walk past the local art gallery and a fountain. It's tempting to throw some money in and make a wish that everything's going to be all right. As I head further along the path, large fig trees provide patches of shady relief from the sun. A couple of blocks more and I'm at my destination. It's a renovated Queenslander nestled between newly built apartment buildings. I slip my phone into my pocket and contemplate my next move.

Taking a deep breath, I stare at the front of the house. Goosebumps ripple across my skin. I tingle all over. Shivering, I take another step forward and knock. A few beats later the wooden door swings open. My "twin" stares back at me. I slip off my sunnies. For a moment her hand clenches into a fist and I'm worried she's going to take a swing at me.

"Can I help you?" Michelle asks, understandably cautious.

I drink her in. She's almost an exact duplicate, but leaner, harder, and much more athletic. She must do some serious exercise. We don't share the same taste in clothes. She's got on skin-tight dark leggings and a black T-shirt.

"Um, I'm sorry to just turn up like this. But I need to talk to you." I resist the urge to look at my shoes. "I think you can see why for yourself."

She glances up and down the street, and then opens the door wider to let me pass into the lounge room. I take a seat on the large couch while Michelle perches on the edge of a recliner. She taps her fingers, impatiently waiting. I pull off my hat and put it beside me with my sunnies inside.

The room is inviting, lots of family pictures including some with a man and a woman whom I'm guessing are her parents. They're both dark-skinned, so Michelle isn't obviously adopted like I am when people see me with my parents. She even has a brother and a sister of the same complexion. I wonder if they are adopted too or the biological children of her parents.

This might be harder than I thought. I stare at a vase with flowers on a small table next to me, my mind racing. I take another deep breath and face my sister. Michelle seems much calmer than I expected, apart from her eyes darting occasionally towards the ceiling.

"I'm sorry. I don't know where to start." My fingers fiddle with a loose thread from my shorts.

"How about you tell me who you are?" Michelle gives me the once over.

"Okay. I'm Mishca." I fumble. "I think we might be sisters."

"Really?" Her eyes narrow. "What makes you think that?"

I wring my hands together. How stupid was I to think I could turn up here like this?

"Um, well, we were both adopted from the same agency for one thing." I struggle to stop fidgeting, but end up curling my hands into fists and releasing them again. "And well, look at us."

A thump from upstairs causes me to flinch.

"Ignore that. It's just my dog falling over. Stupid bitch is lame and needs to be put down."

I swear for a second Michelle smiles. Anxiety rises, tightening my chest, but I can't put my finger on why.

"Do you have any proof? How do I know it's not a scam?" Michelle asks, holding my gaze. She's too calm, pretty unruffled. It doesn't seem right.

This isn't going the way I expected at all. Not that I thought we'd hug and be instant best friends, but I was hoping for a warmer reception than this. Her behavior is so odd. My lie detector doesn't pick anything up, but that doesn't stop me from feeling uneasy. I push the thoughts away. Having your exact double show up would be enough to make anyone act weird.

"I've got files that prove it." I bite my lip, searching for the words to tell her the rest.

"Can I see them?" she asks. It's the most eager she's been since I got here.

Something in the back of my mind twinges. *This is off.* I turn my hands palm up. "Ah, I don't have them with me."

"Well, why don't you come back with them and we can talk some more." Michelle stands up, indicating she wants me to leave.

I rise, but determined to change her mind. "Wait, there's something else. You're in danger, someone's going to try and kill y—"

"Help! Somebody help me!" A voice just like mine screams from upstairs.

My doppelganger's head whips towards me. She grins. "Somebody's trying to kill Michelle. Is that what you were telling me?"

Quicker than I've seen anyone move, my evil twin

rushes to the stairs. Instinctively, I snatch the vase behind me and throw it at her head. It hits her in the temple. She goes down. Hello, superpowers. I rush over, hurdling the unmoving body at the bottom of the stairs and race up.

"I need help!"

I find her in a bedroom tied to a chair that lies sideways on the ground. Blood pools on the floor around her head. A gag sits askew under her chin like she's wiggled it down from her mouth.

"No!" shouts Michelle, her eyes widening at the sight of me.

"Shhh." I put my finger to my lips. "It's okay. I'm not *her*. I'm Mishca. I'm your sister. I'm here to save you."

I race to her. My fingers fumble at the knots. I swallow hard when I see what's laid out on the bed — a spread of knives. "I'm so sorry. I didn't expect them to be after you so soon. I was coming to warn you."

"Who is she? Why do we all look alike?" she pleads.

Pulling Michelle to her feet, I touch my blood kin for the first time ever. "We're sisters. That's all you need to know for now. I'll tell you more when we get somewhere safe."

She lets go and takes a step back. It's so strange to see myself standing in front of me. We're not exact duplicates any more than the one downstairs. Michelle is plumper than me with a rounder face. But still.

"Why does she want to kill me?" Michelle asks, wrapping her arms around her chest.

"You're evidence." My voice threatens to quaver,

but I quell it.

"Evidence of what?"

"Okay, less questioning and more running. I'll explain as soon as I can."

"Evidence of our existence." The voice comes from the doorway. A chill runs up my spine. "*You're* dying, Michelle, and the last thing we need is for someone to perform an autopsy on you."

"I'm dying?" My non-evil sister's eyes bulge. Then the last part of our villainous sibling's words sink in. "What autopsy?"

"Don't want anyone finding that nifty little chip in your head."

Michelle squeals and leaps behind me. A trickle of blood runs down the false Michelle's face. She can't be Tammy, because Tammy's scheduled for termination too. She must be the one healed by Wirth— Phanessa.

"Don't do this, Phanessa. Sh—"

"*Never* call me that!" she screams at me. "That's not my name anymore. I am Othilia."

Othilia, right. I'd forgotten she was renamed.

"Michelle is your sister," I continue, but I somehow doubt I can rationalize with her. I drop my shoulders forward and brace my feet. My body somehow falls into a fighting stance I didn't know I knew. "She's our sister."

"If I had it my way there would only be me." Othilia sneers. "But Wirth thinks you have value." There's so much sarcasm in her words. "She has none. She's dead weight. Move out of my way, so I can finish what I started."

Michelle whimpers.

"No." I stand my ground.

"You're no match for me. I was activated years ago. I'm stronger, faster, and smarter."

"There are two of us against you," I claim with false bravado.

Othilia laughs. "Her? She's never been activated. She's a plain old defective."

Defective. The hospital! Othilia was at the hospital when I met Markus. And that tingling feeling that went through me when I arrived, I had that sensation at the hospital when I overheard her talking. Has she been stalking me all along?

My lapse in concentration is enough for Othilia to charge me. She knocks me down and pins me to the ground with her foot. Her strength is incredible. I struggle for air.

Michelle runs for the door. In one smooth motion, Othilia seizes one of the knives on the bed and throws. It hits Michelle squarely between the shoulder blades. As she crumples to the ground, sadness hits me followed by a tearing pain inside. Othilia and I both scream. I *feel* my sister dying! Her soul being torn from her body pierces my heart.

I curl up as Othilia removes her foot. She grits her teeth and groans, remaining upright despite the obvious pain.

"It's time to go." Othilia's hand clasps me under my armpits. "Can't let you get caught."

She hauls me up. I make a break for downstairs, but Othilia yanks me back with brute strength.

"You're such a pain in the arse. I don't know why Wirth wants you," she snarls, lifting me off my feet. I'm a rag doll, still reeling from the death throes. She lets me go. I collapse in a heap. "Pathetic."

She jerks the knife from Michelle's flesh and fresh blood seeps free. Scooping up her gleaming collection of blades, Othilia shoves them into a bag and slings it over her shoulder.

"Pick her up. I'm sick of raiding morgues for empty shells like her."

It's an order I want to ignore. But I have to think of my other sisters. If I don't stay alive, they're dead for sure too. Othilia moves to Michelle's feet. I squat down and reach through under my lifeless sister's armpits. Her warm blood leaches onto me.

We awkwardly make our way down the stairs. More red trickles over me. As we near the front door she repositions her cargo into one hand and then holds up her fist to signal "freeze." My doppelganger peers through the window at the street and then signals for me to come with the wave of an arm. My body feels as weak as it was pre-op, and I know right now I'm no match for Othilia. I'm not sure how she recovered so fast from Michelle's death. Maybe her training with Wirth has hardened her to the experience. She marches us across the lounge room and through the kitchen. We move towards a door that leads into a garage and then she drops her end of my sister's body to open the door. The car is reversed in, making this easier. I guess she had everything already planned. Othilia lets go again and opens the boot. Michelle's limbs end up splayed in a gauche manner.

Othilia frog-marches me around the car, opens the passenger door, and shoves me in, banging my head on metal in the process. There's no blood, but a lump forms quickly and a grey blur clouds my vision. My eyes hurt as she opens the garage door and the light streams in.

I bury my head in my hands while we drive off. A mix of emotions course through me, grief for Michelle and fear of Othilia. I was so close. If I had been a few hours earlier, I could have saved her. I take a peek across at my assailant. We're meant to be copies of the same person, but right now, I don't recognize her as someone I could be related to at all.

I clutch the side of my seat, wondering if there's a chance to escape from this mad woman. She's faster and stronger than me. I definitely need the element of surprise. I release my grip, leaving a scarlet print.

"Why aren't you called Phanessa anymore?" I ask, hoping to distract her.

"Do you know what that name means?" She sneers. "It's Greek for butterfly — a weak fragile creature with a short lifespan. Once Wirth healed and activated me, that was no longer a fitting name. I was reborn as Othilia — rich battle." She seems to stand taller as though she's proud of what our maker has turned her into. "I was made to fight and now I am a warrior in every aspect. If you're lucky, he'll rename you too. Though I don't know why he'd bother."

As my mind sizes up a possible escape route, Othilia pulls over and leans past me to open the door.

"He's got plans for you and he'll come for what's his soon enough." Othilia shoves me from her car. "I'd take you to him, but I've got other people to kill."

CHAPTER 10

RYDER

EVERY FIBER OF MY BEING wants to run after Mishca. She should not have to do this alone, but that is the way she wants it. Instead Nerissa and Dylan walk towards the local shopping center with me tagging along as the third wheel. A block away from our destination my counterparts stare off to the right—a swimming lagoon, way better option than shopping.

"Do you guys want to go in?" The water is so inviting, despite the cooler temperature and the butt-load of kids in there screaming each time the giant bucket dumps water on them at the wet playground area.

Nerissa and Dylan gape at each other over something I am obviously missing.

"If you want to go for a swim we'll just lay here, I don't have my bikini with me." Nerissa twirls a lock of blond hair around her finger.

"Well, you could get one from the shopping center." I gesture to the giant car park across the road.

"Pfft," Dylan says. "Like she needs more clothes." His fiancé punches him playfully.

The three of us walk through the concrete entrance. To our right is the kiddie area — the very noisy kiddie area — but up the area to the left is packed. We walk across the wooden bridge and set up on the other side of the lagoon on a grassy patch.

Dylan and Nerissa get under a large umbrella that a family vacated only moments before. The two of them lay back in the shade. It is a good spot, tucked away near the side fence, abutting the car park. I peel off my shirt and toss it on the ground beside them and then stride over to the lagoon's edge.

The area where I have entered is so shallow that I have to tread a fair way before it is deep enough for me to dive in. I find an area not occupied by many people and flip over onto my back, letting the water cover me as I float. Staring at the sky, my mind drifts from Mishca to my mother. Confusion thuds at me with each heartbeat. *I need to talk to Sophitia.* The waves of emotion that flowed to me from my mother when she said goodbye have never left me. She had a good reason and it broke her heart. But it was not Rosie.

We should be back in Brisbane in a week or so, depending on how long it takes with Mishca's sisters, and then I will track my cousin down and this puzzle will be solved.

Mishca's sisters.

I let my feet find the concrete floor of the lagoon. Right now, Mishca is probably trying to explain to a complete stranger that they are not simply relatives, but exact duplicates of another person and there is a madman out to get them.

I should have gone with her.

My gaze falls on Nerissa and Dylan. The two of them lay side by side, seemingly enjoying the shadow cast over them, but Nerissa regards the water like a long lost lover. Dylan is such a spoilsport. Children beside me squeal and splash around, catching me with wayward droplets. I let the playfulness of the day seep into my skin like the warmth of the sun. Some fun is exactly what we need right now.

Something moves on the other side of the fence, between two vehicles in the car park. I peer closer, but see nothing.

"Hey, guys. Come on in," I call.

Nerissa is in shorts and a blue top, it will be easy for her to get changed back at the motel, and Dylan is in quick-dry board shorts so it is not really a problem for him either. The Mackay weather makes it feel like it is not even winter today, more like spring.

"No, we're fine," Dylan calls back, shaking his head. But Nerissa continues to stare at the water.

I grin to myself. We need to lighten up and have some fun. I wait until they turn away and then sneak towards them. Nerissa and Dylan are so deep in conversation that they do not notice my approach.

"I don't want to do this, Dylan. It doesn't feel right," Nerissa says as I tiptoe towards her.

"I understand, but you have to. You know the consequences if you don't," Dylan replies. "There's so much more at stake here—"

He stops short seeing me behind Nerissa. I reach down and scoop Nerissa up in my arms, bolting toward the water.

"Dylan!" she cries with an unexpected edge of urgency. People turn around at the commotion.

I slow my pace as she thrashes in my arms. It is like she thinks I am attacking her. She slips from my grasp and onto the ground. Dylan storms over, grabbing a random navy and white striped towel hanging off a nearby chair. Wrapping it around her body, he holds her close and rubs his hands up and down her arms reassuringly.

"Hey, I am sorry. I did not mean to freak her—"

Before I can finish, Dylan's fist slams into my jaw. Pain sparks through my bones. Something inside me stirs, wanting to strike. Instead I rub my chin and focus on my breath. He lifts Nerissa into his arms and marches off. I gather up our stuff and trail after them.

"Oi. Come on, man. It was just some fun," I call. Okay, I totally had a brain fart, but this reaction is over the top.

Before I can catch up with them, an ominous security guard blocks Dylan. I place our things on the ground, unsure of what is about to happen.

"Right, you three," he points to us and then throws his hand towards the exit. "You're out of here."

"Gladly," Dylan says through clenched teeth. He continues to hold Nerissa tight as he storms off. Nerissa's eyes stay on me, her face contorted in anguish. Under the watchful eyes of the security guard, I gather our stuff and push my way through the stream of families coming into the lagoon.

Dylan marches on, backtracking the route to the motel, not even breaking stride to put Nerissa down. She bounces around in his arms, her head buried into the nape of his neck.

"Nerissa, I am sorry. It was meant to be a joke, some fun," I shout, striding to shorten the distance between us.

When they reach the corner of the car park, Nerissa squirms.

"Dylan, put me down." She pushes against his chest. "It's not his fault. He doesn't know."

"Know what?" I ask.

Dylan lowers her to the ground, but continues to eye me.

"Ryder?" Mishca steps from between two cars.

I flinch at the pain in her voice, and when I whip around towards her, my body twitches at the sight of her tear-swollen eyes and the red stains matted across her face and clothing. My tattoos burn and the sensation flows across the rest of my skin. The familiar sparking between my fingers erupts. I need to get it under control. I close my eyes and take deep breaths. *Not here, not now.*

Beside me, Dylan and Nerissa audibly register their shock, but I can barely tell who says what with the effort I am making to stay calm. One last inhale and the feeling dissipates.

"Mishca, what happened?" I ask, my gaze continuing to search for some clue.

Mishca stares at me. "She killed Michelle."

CHAPTER 11

MISHCA

I RISE FROM MY HIDING space, disgusted for finding refuge in such a gross spot. It's an old toilet block at the back of a church. Blue paint is peeling off the walls and it smells musty. I'm so sick of crying, but I've never seen anyone die before. And it was my sister. I was so close to having someone connected to me by blood. Then there was the fear of the police. If they found me at the scene, looking like Michelle and covered in her blood? There would be some serious questions to answer. If they guess who and what I am, I don't know what would happen. One scenario I have trouble shaking is being shipped off to a government lab for testing. I groan at my paranoia and search inside for the strength to walk.

I push down the rage and sorrow threatening to overtake me again, numbing myself to it all. *Harden up, princess.* I have no idea how long I've been here attempting to make sense of what happened. But I realize that there's no more time to waste. I need to get to Andrea and Tammy. And I need to find Ryder.

My chest hurts from where Othilia stood on me. My breathing isn't labored anymore, but I can still feel where her boot pressed against me. I check my location on Maps. It's only a couple of blocks to the water park. If they're not there, I'll have to text them. There's no way I could talk on the phone without falling to pieces. Even texting feels like an effort right now.

People peer at me strangely, like they know I'm a freak. My hat and sunnies are still at Michelle's, so I keep my head down, focusing on the blue dot of my location and the red dot of my destination.

It doesn't take long for me to arrive at the water park. The Bluewater Lagoon is filled with locals and tourists. It's one place that's bustling and full of life. I feel like a deviant, lurking in the bushes, scouring the crowd for my friends. Nerissa and Dylan are sunbathing on a grassy patch. Then, I spot Ryder in the water, squealing children splashing all around him.

The best thing would be for Ryder to see me so I can signal to him, but he keeps glancing at our friends until they turn away. Then he sneaks from the water towards them. When he's right beside Nerissa, he swoops in and scoop her up in his arms, bolting for the water.

A whole lot of yelling ensures. Nerissa slips from his grasp. Her skin shimmers oddly where she has come into contact with his wet body. Is that her secret? But before I can get a better view, Dylan wraps a large towel around her and then advances on Ryder. I only see his clenched fist right before it connects with

Ryder's jaw. Dylan strides away carrying Nerissa. The haze of shock takes over again and Michelle's lifeless body flashes before my eyes. Bile rises in my throat.

I open my eyes to search for my friends, but they're lost in the crowd. A family pulls into a car park near me. I scoot further into the bushes. They bustle past me without a sideways glance. Peering through the foliage, I spot my friends again. They're coming towards me on the footpath.

"Ryder?" I step from my sanctuary.

The three of them twist around towards me. I catch my reflection in a car window: puffy eyes and blood smeared on my hands and clothes. Dylan swears, and Nerissa gasps. For a moment, Ryder emanates a faint blue glow like he did in my room.

"Mishca, what happened?" he asks, searching my face for clues.

"She killed Michelle." My voice is void of emotion. Everything feels numb.

"Who killed Michelle?" Nerissa asks, touching my shoulder.

"My sister."

"Whoa, slow down a minute." Dylan holds his hands in front of him. "We didn't sign up for this." He turns to Nerissa. "Your father put you in my care and I'm not going to let you be put in danger."

"Dylan, you don't understand," Nerissa pleads.

"Don't understand what? That Mishca has a psycho birth family? I think I got that." He shoots me a dirty look that reminds me of Fin. Then, his words sink in. She hasn't told him.

Ryder ushers me to a spare park beside a 4WD and pulls my top off. "This is something to talk about later. Right now, we need to get Mishca cleaned up." He pours a bottle of water over me and Nerissa uses the towel to wipe me down.

I can't see evidence of any shimmering skin. Maybe my eyes were playing tricks on me, part of the shock.

"Mishca can't go around like that," Dylan says pragmatically, gesturing to my state of half-undress.

The white panels of towel have random red blooms over them, obviously not part of any pattern.

"Ryder, you stay here with Mishca. Dylan and I will go to the shops and get a dress." Nerissa clasps her fiancé's hand and tugs him towards the shopping center before he can protest.

I retreat to the garden bed and crouch down, hoping no one notices my dishevelled and bloody state.

"Are you okay?" Ryder asks before swearing. "Sorry, that was the stupidest question in the world. I meant, did she hurt you?"

I wipe my red palms on my jeans, but my sister's blood just gets smeared around instead. Too much of the bodily fluid already coats my clothes for them to make any difference. "Not bad. But there's something else. Remember how I told you that I used to get these attacks, and that's how they discovered my heart problem, but we never found out what the go was with the episodes?"

"Yes."

"They were my sisters dying." Ryder's jaw goes slack. "It hit me when Michelle died. I had one the day we…broke up. That must have been sister number five Connor referred to before."

"How did you get away?"

"She let me go. Wirth told her she can't hurt me, and she obviously doesn't see me as a threat, or couldn't take me on the road with her."

I can't look at Ryder. The guilt of Colin, of the dead person's heart in my chest, of me being alive when so many of my clone sisters are dead overwhelms me. Something inside me wants to break, but I turn to steel instead. Hard, cold, tough, and silent.

It's as if Ryder knows I need this quiet time. He says nothing. He just takes my hand and strokes my thumb. We stay hidden in the garden until Nerissa and Dylan return.

"It's not very fashionable." Nerissa slides a long-sleeved orange dress from a plastic bag.

Not exactly my color, but I don't care. I tug it on, eager to cover my bra. As it falls over my hips, I unbutton my jeans and wrench them down. They leave fresh smears of blood that need to be washed off. I'm not spotless, but I'm good enough to head to the hotel without having the front desk call the police on us.

Dylan pipes up as we make our way back towards our accommodation. "So is someone going to fill me in?"

"It's not my birth family. It's something else." I take a deep breath. "I wouldn't expect you to understand."

"All I know is that we shouldn't even be here in the first place." He raises his voice and Ryder moves towards him, but I press a hand to Ryder's chest to halt his momentum.

"Dylan!" Nerissa protests, causing passers-by to stop and stare. "I told you that Mishca was going through something really rough."

"Nothing justifies treating your best friend like that." He rounds on me. "Of putting her in danger."

"Wait up a minute," Ryder interjects. "Mishca went through hell and — "

"And she decided to bring Nerissa with her?" Dylan folds his arms.

"No," Nerissa says. "I volunteered because I don't abandon friends." She turns to me. "What are you going to do now?"

"I have to get to the others. We need to leave. She's going to kill Andrea and Tammy."

"No way." Dylan waves his hands like a baseball umpire calling a batter out. "We're going back to Brisbane."

"Mishca, tell him. He'll understand." Nerissa's eyes plead with me as much as her voice.

"Roger, but not here."

Dylan and Nerissa fall a few steps behind, whispering to each other in heated tones. I know if I wanted to I could probably hear what they're saying, but I'm exhausted.

When Ryder goes to slip his hand into mine, he zaps me with static electricity. My arm jolts and a weird giggle escapes me that relieves some of the tension. Our hands find each other again. My palm and heart warm. The last few hours were like a nightmare, far worse than any of the control dreams that had been implanted in my head.

I have to pull myself together for Tammy and Andrea. I'm their only hope.

We stop to cross the street, and Ryder wipes at my face one last time. He stuffs the bloodstained towel into the bag before we enter the lobby. The wait for the elevator is infuriating. I tap my foot. It finally pings open for us and we step in, acting casual. I sag with relief when the doors finally close.

"Dylan, look at me." Nerissa places her hands on his face and makes him face her. "You will understand when you hear what Mishca has to say. Listen to her, and then decide if you want to go back to Brisbane. But understand I *will* be going to Airlie and Townsville with Mishca."

He glares at me. His funky mood can't override how grateful I am for Nerissa right now. No way I want to tackle Townsville alone.

We all stand like statues on the elevator ride up, staring at the floor numbers tick above the door until it opens. Ryder strides towards our room, casting a wary glance over his shoulder.

Once inside, Dylan turns on me straight away with anger bubbling just below the surface. "So spill, what's so important that you ignored Nerissa, making her cry her eyes red, and then got you chasing around some long lost sisters with a psycho running around who wants to kill them?"

Ryder sits on the bed beside me, squeezing my hand.

I take a deep breath. "You know that Nerissa helped me find my adoption records."

Dylan nods. "It was before that you gave her the cold shoulder for a week."

Nerissa elbows him. "You said you wanted to hear it, so shut up."

I clear my voice and continue, "Well, we discovered I don't have any birth parents because I was never born. I was created. I'm a clone."

"Whoa, what?" Dylan takes a couple of steps back.

"A clone. Mishca found out that night she was made in a test tube." Ryder puffs his chest like he's expecting some fist-cuff action. "You got a problem with that?"

"Can you imagine how hard it would be for someone to learn that?" Nerissa whispers. "It's why she cut herself off from me. Well, from everyone." She gestures to Ryder. "How does someone live with the burden of that knowledge, keeping it a secret from friends and family?"

Something in her voice sounds like she's talking about more than just me here. I guess she feels a kinship to me. I have my secret and she has her secret betrothed status with Dylan. She may have another one yet too. I'd bet on it.

"Is this for real?" Dylan's voice reflects the stunned horror I felt that night of the cloning facility break-in. He glances between us.

"It's true. As much as I wish that it wasn't." I wrap my arms around my chest. "Believe me, I wish this wasn't real."

Nerissa puts her hand on Dylan's arm. "We'll talk more about it later."

As though it's some secret language between them, he loses his rigid stance and then takes her hand and brings it to his lips. He may have accepted what I am, but he isn't convinced that we should be doing this.

"What about the fact we're probably walking straight into another murder scene in Airlie or Townsville?" Dylan turns his gaze from me to Nerissa. "How can I let you be in that danger?"

"How can you expect me to leave a friend in danger? Mishca's sisters are being hunted. *Hunted.*"

Again, there's something more happening between them than the words spoken. Maybe it has something to do with Nerissa's secret. I brush away the thought. We have bigger things to worry about now.

He softens. "Okay, we'll go. But Mishca, I have to come to protect you and Nerissa."

"Sure thing, beefcake." Ryder smirks, rubbing his jaw.

"But one thing," Dylan says, ignoring the snide remark. "Why does someone want to kill your sisters? And why don't they want to kill you?"

I give him the rundown of the lab, what we know about my reason for existing in the first place, and how the "defective" clones are being disposed of to hide the evidence of their creation. I don't mention the bit where Ryder, Nerissa, and the others got knocked unconscious, and that we don't know how we managed to end up back home.

A swear word escapes Dylan's lips in a whisper at

the end of my tale. He sits immobilized on the lounge.

"Mishca, I'm so sorry. I had no idea. That would be enough for anyone to have a meltdown." Nerissa moves closer to him, squeezing his hand. He turns to her. "Why didn't you tell me?"

"It isn't my secret to tell. You know that. Everyone has a part of themselves locked away deep inside. Something they never want to see the light of day. Maybe if I wasn't there with her, I would never have known. I wouldn't blame someone for keeping the fact they're a clone a secret. It's huge." Her voice is raw.

He stands up and walks over to Ryder, hand extended. "You protected my girl. You guys couldn't have known what you would find there. Thanks."

"No problem, man," Ryder says. They grip each other's hands.

'Why not go to the cops with all this?" Dylan asks as they let go.

"And have Mishca whisked off to some secret government dissection table?" Ryder leans against the wall, arms folded." Or worse?"

What's worse? I wonder, but decide not to think about it. I hop off the bed and pace. I wasn't able to save Michelle, but I can't stand the thought of failing Tammy and Andrea as well.

"They're in danger. We need to get to them now." I eye my phone. "Let's get the hire van. I think if we leave now we'll get some time on Othilia. She's got to dispose of the body and I think she's driving too."

"Okay, but you stay by me." Dylan cups Nerissa's chin and lifts her face towards his. "If your dad ever finds out, he'll kill me himself."

Nerissa worries her lip between her teeth.

A sense of relief washes over me. "Let's get going. The sooner we get moving, the sooner we'll know the others are safe."

CHAPTER 12

RYDER

DYLAN AND I WAIT OUTSIDE the car rental office as Nerissa and Mishca finalize the paperwork. The heat bears down on us, prickling my skin. Like Mishca, I cannot wait to leave this city and keep on with our mission. The sooner we get her sisters safe, the sooner I can get some answers from Sophitia. It is not a conversation to have over the phone or via a message.

While Dylan may say he is cool with everything that has gone down, I worry it is an act. I certainly would not be comfortable if he and Mishca shared a secret that I was not privy to. Maybe that is me projecting my insecurities onto him. And then there was his overreaction with me over Nerissa. Since when did pretending to throw someone in a pool qualify as a punchable offense? I trust Nerissa. She has proven herself a friend. But her boyfriend is another story.

"Hey, man." Dylan casts a look at the girls before returning his gaze to me. "While I totally understand you keeping the secret for your girl," I quirk an eyebrow at his seeming mind-reading ability, "tell me now if there's anything else I need to know. I can't keep her safe if I'm in the dark."

For a moment I am caught. He would definitely want to know about me being able to get my blue-glow freak on. But the words "need to know" give me an out. "Nope, you have everything you need to know. Mishca discovered she was created through cloning, not born. Her creator is making a private army and wants her back to be part of it. He has ordered the execution of her remaining clone sisters because of their unrepaired heart defects, but Mishca is not going to let that happen." I pause thinking of Michelle. "Well, she is trying not to let that happen."

He gives me a nod, appearing satisfied with my response. A knot that had formed in my stomach uncurls. I have never been a good liar. I can withhold things no problem, almost talk in riddles so I am technically telling the truth. But straight lying is not something I do.

Nerissa emerges holding onto a set of keys, her face set hard, a stark contrast to the bubbly version of her that dangled the hotel room key yesterday. So much has changed in less than twenty-four hours. Mishca follows her best friend with a matching expression. She comes over and laces her fingers with mine.

"Let's do this," she says with a steely determination.

We pack up and check out with raised eyebrows from the staff at reception. Everything has been such a whirlwind since we left Brisbane that I have barely had time to focus on what it means that my mother was not my mother, and that Sophitia knows the truth. But with Mishca focused on driving and saving Andrea, and the lovebirds canoodling in the back, my mind wanders to my cousin. I yank my phone from my pocket and tap a text expressing the need to talk when we return without stating that I know she is my cousin. I intend to learn more about Coen and Adair as well. Although I am not certain they were talking about me that night at the club, given the crazy shit that has been happening, I am not taking any chances.

***

Our van chugs along the main street of Airlie Beach, the footpaths beside us are filled with tanned holidaymakers. It took us less than two hours to get here so I pray it is enough of a head start on Mishca's deranged sister.

I regret going for the cheapest option, which sees us in a clapped people mover with a unicorn painted on the side and no air-conditioning. Sweat forms in so many unsexy places on everyone. *Come on. It is supposed to be winter. Why is it so warm?*

"I think we've gone past the turn-off." Mishca grips the steering wheel even tighter in frustration.

"Hang on. I will check the map." I click on my phone and follow the blue line from us to our next destination, Andrea's house. "You can take the next right."

She flicks on the indicator and then turns onto the street, the van chugging up a hill. There are no touristy shops here, but there are a lot of flashy houses. We stop a couple of blocks away from the address that Connor gave us on the off chance Othilia's around. I count along the houses to determine the right one and see a large white home that rivals Mishca's place in Brisbane, minus the giant gate. The house seems lifeless, but with one this size people could easily be inside without us being able to see them from the street.

"Do you want us to come too?" Nerissa asks.

"No." Mishca unclicks her seatbelt. "Othilia might already be in there. It's best if I go up alone."

"Not a chance." I open my car door, snatching a cap and shoving it on. I pull it down tightly so that I can only just see under the brim. Mishca grips a pair of oversized sunglasses and puts a scarf over her hair. "We left Mackay straight away and I think it would have taken her longer, you know."

She glances at me with uncertainty before sliding the sunglasses on. The two of us walk along the footpath until we reach the house. I will my legs to keep my pace steady as we make our way up the tiled stairs towards a large wooden door. Mishca seems to gulp before pressing the bell.

She puts her ear to the door.

"Anything?" I ask.

"No." She knocks on the door hard. "I normally can feel my sisters. I've learned to recognize a tingling sensation. But I feel nothing, which means no Andrea, and no Othilia either." She pauses. "Wait. Someone is coming."

"Andrea? What on earth are you doing?" a voice calls from behind us. We all freeze.

CHAPTER 13

MISHCA

I SPIN AROUND TO SEE an elderly lady making her way gingerly up the stairs, gripping the handrail tight. She holds fast to a wad of envelopes in her other hand.

"I—ah." Words fail me. I strike a mental uppercut for not picking up a potential threat earlier, avoiding this interaction altogether.

"I thought you weren't back until the end of February. Surely Europe wasn't that boring that you decided to come home early." She peers at me through thick glasses.

"I'll be joining them soon. I had to, um," I gawk at Ryder for inspiration, "visit some friends." That sounds so lame and unrealistic, but I don't know what else to tell her.

"So I'll still collect the mail and water the plants then?" she asks.

"Yes, please."

"You've changed your hair again." The old lady hands me the mail. "It looks nice. Pop these on the mantel then."

"Oh, ah, I've lost my key," I lie. Who lies to little old ladies? Better than explaining the truth.

"Again? Oh dear." She proceeds to tisk at me. I just totally got scolded. She shuffles up to the door and unlocks it.

"Thanks." I slip past her with Ryder in tow. A set of keys hangs on a hook inside the door. I snatch them up. "Oh look, here they are. No need to worry."

She beams at us. "That's good. When are you leaving?"

"Probably tomorrow if everything goes to plan."

"Don't do anything I wouldn't do," she cackles, winking at us. "Don't worry. I won't dob you in to your parents. As hard as it may be for you to believe, I was young once too."

I stay at the door, watching her until she is in her own yard and back inside her house. I get Ryder to text Nerissa and Dylan to rendezvous. The two of them slink from the car and run up to the house in the least covert way possible. Honestly, I want to slap their heads together.

"What's going on?" Nerissa asks with a nervous edge to her voice.

"Andrea is on holiday." Ryder continues to scout the neighbourhood for possible danger.

"Good, we'll get going." Dylan turns towards the van.

"Not yet." I take off my scarf and sunnies. No real need to hide my appearance now. "I want to have a look around first."

"Okay, we'll go wait in the car in case any crazed Mishca doppelgangers turn up." Dylan sinks back into his seat.

Nerissa glares at him, but doesn't protest. "Be careful."

"Here, can you stash these back in the van?" I pass over my lame disguise props. Last thing I want to do is accidently put them down somewhere and leave them.

Nerissa and Dylan rush off down the stairs.

The inside foyer is white marble with bronze features everywhere. At the end of the room is an arced internal staircase, leading up to a balcony that seems to be the midpoint of a hallway. That's where I want to go.

"What do you want to find?" Ryder follows close on my heels.

"Something about my sister." I let my hand glide over the cool metal surface of the banister. Instinctively, I know Andrea's room is to the right. Not the first room, but the second. Standing in her doorway, I scan the room for any clues to what she's like. The walls are a muted peach and the bed is made with dark orange sheets. A music stand is off in the corner with a violin case propped against the window beside it.

I push away the trespassing guilt, walk over to her wardrobe, and glide the door open.

"You both share the same shoe fetish." Ryder laughs at the pile inside.

I poke my tongue at him. Rolling the door across, I peek in the other side. There are no more shoes, but plenty of clothes. A blue box catches my attention high on a top shelf. Even on tiptoe, I can't reach it.

"Could you get that down for me?" I point to it.

"I could, but would I?" Ryder winks.

Seriously! Grammar jokes at a time like this? You think I'd be used to them by now from him. My hands go to my hips. I shoot him my best "I'm not impressed" look. He holds up his arms, surrendering.

"Okay. I will stop now." He laughs again, reaching up and pulling the box down for me.

I seize it and put in on the bed, swiftly pulling the lid off. Inside is a bunch of letters addressed to Eleithyia Elite Family Services that have been returned to sender, a birth certificate, and some newspaper clippings. I pick the first one up and peer at it. It's social shots from a beach volleyball charity competition in Mackay. I can't see anything significant, so I lay it on the bed.

Ryder takes a photo scrapbook that was on the shelf beside the box and goes through it.

"Her hair color is different." He turns the book towards me, pointing to a photo. Andrea is holding onto her violin and a trophy. Her hair is darker than mine with shots of red through it.

I hold the next clipping in my fingertips and am just as confused. More social shots, this time of high school dance. I scan the names in case I'm missing something, but nothing stands out. Frustrated, I put it with the other one. Ryder swaps the scrapbook for the clippings and stares intently.

"Mishca, here." His finger points to the

background.

It's a bit blurred, but there's me, well one of my sisters, behind a group of guys posing at the volleyball tournament.

Snatching up the high school dance one, I quickly spot me again. They're both from Mackay papers. *Michelle*. Andrea found Michelle. There's a bunch of them with her floating around in the background, but eventually, I find a clipping of her doing a piano recital at a local music competition. I check the dates. They're all from the last couple of months.

I rifle through the remaining contents of the box. There are some notes in a handwriting that matches mine. It includes Michelle's address and a speech that shows Andrea was planning to visit her once she got back from Europe. She thought she'd found her twin sister.

"How long has Andrea lived here?" I ask, racking my brain for the information from the files.

"Not long. Less than six months. She was from Sydney before that." Ryder holds up a drama book and points. "I remember thinking how lucky we were that she had moved here."

Sadness squiggles through my veins, the shared interest a stabbing reminder of the normal life I've lost.

"Trying to juggle visits to two states would have been—" The sensation I've learned to dread washes over me, making me cut off my words. She's close and moving fast. I can hear the pounding of her footsteps up the stairs. I push Ryder into the wardrobe and slide the door shut.

"Oh. It's you." Othilia sneers at me from the doorway. She's dressed in black leggings, knee-high boots, and a tight black T-shirt, her hair tied in a ponytail. Could she be anymore cliché?

She advances and I flatten against the wall opposite the wardrobe. I have a clear view of it now and her back is to it.

"If only I could kill you." She sighs. "Maybe I should and tell Wirth it was an accident."

I fix my gaze on Othilia as behind her a blue glow emanates from Ryder's hiding spot along with a low-frequency hum.

She grins, oblivious to Ryder, too caught up in trying to connect a fist with my face. I barely manage to duck. Her hand crunches into the wall. She blows the peach dust off her knuckles, and then without warning, kicks at my stomach. My hands clutch her leg as she connects. Twisting my arms, I manage to flip her onto the ground and leap on top of her, striking at her head. She blocks me easily and kicks me back off.

She reaches into her right boot and grips a knife then waves it at me in a taunting fashion me. "Guess I'll have to kill you the same way I killed your sister."

"Wait," I cry, feebly stalling while the military side of my mind searches for a strategy. *Don't fail me now!* A weak idea, but if it works... "I thought Wirth wanted me alive."

"He does, but I can always lie."

She raises her arm, but a bolt of blue light hits her before she releases the knife. It clatters to the floor, bloodless, like her body. Ryder bursts from the wardrobe, still glowing, and seizes my hand.

"Come on!" he yells as I move towards Othilia, desperate to find a pulse.

"But what if she's dead?" I plead. "She's still my blood."

Othilia groans.

"Is that good enough for you?" Ryder cocks a brow.

My temporary insanity ends. She's a remorseless killer. *She's not like you. And you're not like her. She's not your sister, just some crazy chick grown from the same cells as you.* But maybe I should be like her.

I stride over and pick up her knife.

"Mishca, what are you doing?"

"Ending this." My hands and voice shake. Her blade gleams in the sunlight streaming through the window. She killed Michelle. She will kill Tammy and Andrea. This is the only way.

My gaze flickers from her chest to her throat to her leg as I ponder if I should slice at the aorta, femoral, or carotid artery. Or maybe I should go straight for her heart. Tears slide down my face. I don't want to do this. But what other option is there?

"Mishca, please. This is not you." Ryder puts a hand on my shoulder. "There is another way." He pulls a satin sash from a dressing gown and hands it to me. "Tap into your soldier side for knot tying, not stabbing."

I wince at his words. The knife slips from my fingers. I want to bury my face in my hands and sob, but this is not the time. Sash in hand, I expertly bind Othilia, hands behind her back. She moans as I slide her over towards the bed.

"I need something else." I rummage through a chest of drawers and only find T-shirts and shorts.

Ryder hunts around in the wardrobe and comes back with belts and ribbon things. "Will these do?"

"Yep." I take the accessories and put them to a very different use, tying my sister's limbs to the bottom of the bed.

"That should hold her." Ryder reaches for me. "Time to go."

I let him pull me from the room like we're running from a ticking time bomb. Our feet stomp down the stairs and seconds later the door slams behind us. We rush to the car. It's already running with Dylan in the driver's seat. Nerissa has the side door open for us. Before she gets it closed, the tires squeal in protest and the van lurches forward.

"Is she coming?" Nerissa cries, staring out the back of the van.

"I don't think so." I breathe deeply to lower my heart rate.

"We saw her pull up and thought you were both done for." Dylan keeps his head forward as though he doesn't want to be distracted from his task of getting us the heck away from Othilia.

A good thing too. The last thing we need is to have an accident fleeing the scene of a crime.

"How did you manage to get away?" Nerissa asks.

"Mishca distracted her and I managed to get the jump on her." The awe in Ryder's voice surprises me. The tinge of fear does not.

"Really?" Nerissa sounds shocked. "Even with her super strength Mishca wasn't able to take her at Michelle's."

"I got her in the back of the neck. Sometimes it is not how hard you hit, it is where you hit."

I bite my lip at the deception. It's not a full lie, but I can see why Ryder's keeping this to himself. If I had my way, my friends would've never known about my abnormalities. And I would have been oblivious to the facts that I'm a clone, my sisters are dying, and I'm really a soldier for a war that I don't even understand. My craziness is enough to deal with. He can keep his secrets.

CHAPTER 14

RYDER

MY HANDS STILL TINGLE from the lightning blast that zapped Othilia. That has never happened before. Something I definitely have to ask Sophitia about, and hopefully my real mother when we meet. I can skip straight over the "why did you not want me" conversation, because I know she did, and straight onto the "did you give me up to keep me safe because I am some science experiment" question. Though "why in the heck does some other lady think she is my mother" needs to be in there too. I am confident I can get answers from Sophitia.

I have always clung to the memory of that goodbye and was sure it meant my origins are not like Mishca's, but now I am not so sure. For the past few years I could glow and levitate, and that freaked me out big time. But I long ago accepted that there were parts of my life that would remain unknown until I met my mother. I have so many more questions. I have come to the conclusion my adoption was fake. All sorts of scenarios run through my head. Maybe I am like Fin, maybe it was my mother who was experimented on and her powers were passed on to me. Thinking of Fin sets my teeth on edge.

"Are you okay?" Mishca's voice snaps me from my funk.

"I am now." My hand finds hers.

The van decelerates as Nerissa pulls into a service station. Dust rises up from the dirt between the side of the road and the concrete parking area.

"Where are we?" I ask, realizing I completely zoned when we left Airlie.

"Not far from Bowen." Nerissa opens the driver's door. "Still a couple of hours to go, but my bladder won't wait that long."

"Do you two want anything?" Dylan asks as he alights from the passenger side.

"We're all right," Mishca answers for both of us. As soon as they are out of earshot she lowers her voice. "You're so not fine."

"Depends on how you define it." I can always find a loophole. "Being with you makes me happy. My fingers shooting blue laser light, not so much."

"That hasn't happened before?"

"Nope. Just a basic light show with levitation thrown in." I cough to steady my voice so it does not betray my uncertainty. "I had this weird feeling right before the light shot free. It was like pins and needles amplified. I have only had that once before. When we found the facility and had their security on our tail."

"I certainly can't do that, so I think we can stick with your theory that you're not actually linked to

Wirth's experiments." Mishca taps her fingers against the window. "Sophitia should have some answers."

And my mother. I have yet to tell Mishca my firm view that I can still find my real mother. I have been too busy processing that the woman I met was not her.

"How about we get through this week first and we will take it from there?" I do my best to sound reassuring even though doubt plagues my mind. "How are you holding up?"

Instead of answering, Mishca slides closer and presses her lips to mine. My tension drops and I lose myself in her kiss. She grips my shirt while my hands find her face, cupping her chin. My left hand slides down her neck and around to the edge of her hairline, keeping us locked together.

As quickly as the kiss begins, it ends too soon. Mishca inclines her head towards Dylan and Nerissa who are heading back towards us. She smirks.

"What was that for?" I ask.

"You seem to keep me as myself. After the cuddlefest in the motel room I felt more grounded, more normal, less soldier-freak. It's like my programming took an R&R. It's still there, but it's not as aggressive."

"So in other words, we should have as much physical contact as possible." I waggle my eyebrows at her.

She laughs and kisses me lightly. But there is something in her eyes that makes me pause. Fear.

"Can't leave you two alone for five minutes, can we?" Nerissa sniggers.

Mishca turns to her best friend and laughs. My hand grips the seat. *What is going on with her?*

"Like you can talk." Mishca snorts. "How about I drive?"

"Sounds good." Dylan dangles the keys as though he is going to toss them to her.

Mishca and I file from the back of the van while our companions wait to move in. As soon as Mishca's feet hit the ground the keys make a graceful arc in the air from Dylan to her. We waste no time taking up the new seating arrangements. The moment all seatbelts are clicked in, Mishca's foot is on the accelerator. It does not take long for the rocking of the van to lull Dylan and Nerissa to sleep.

"I thought you would want to stay in the back and get all snuggly," I whisper even though Dylan's snores are clearly audible from the back seat.

"I know," she replies with a sigh. "But there's more than just my programming plaguing me. I'm hoping driving will allow me to focus on something other than what's been happening."

"How is that working out for you so far?" I ask.

"Helps a little, but it's not stopping my mind from wandering to what's ahead —a girl unaware that death is coming for her."

That somber note puts an end to the conversation. With Mishca staring straight ahead, steely determination on her face, my eyelids soon droop. When I open them again the sun winks out from behind mountains on the horizon. We must not be far away. The noise coming from the back seat indicates

Dylan still slumbers.

The glare from the setting sun is not helping. I rub my sore eyes and then glance over at Mishca. She takes a swig of an energy drink.

"Those are bad for you," I say with a tisk.

"Hey, sleepyhead." She places the can back in the cup holder.

"How far are we?" I survey our surroundings.

"Not far. We passed a Townsville Regional Council area sign earlier. I think thirty minutes or so. But don't take my word for it. I'm bad at judging driving distances and times. My family always flies for holidays."

"Hmmm." I stare off. All this talk of family makes me wish I had made more moves to mend the bridges better with my dad before I left. Despite our philosophical differences, he raised me and nothing will change that, even when I solve the mystery of my birth mother.

"So are you excited for when we get back?" Mishca's voice cuts through my thoughts.

"Sure, it will be nice to be back home."

"No, that's not what I mean. I meant grilling Sophitia and finding the truth."

She glances at me and then back at the road. This is a topic I have avoided for fear of upsetting Mishca. She will never get a happily-ever-after in that department. I still have that chance.

"I am so nervous. I need answers."

"Sophitia will tell you now that I've spilled the beans, I'm sure of it. She loves you, like I do."

Warmth spreads across my chest at her words. "I love you too." I reach over to take her hand. I give it a squeeze, and then leave my hand resting on her thigh. My fingers feel on fire where they touch her and the sensation spreads up my arm.

Her whole body jolts. I withdraw my hand. Her gaze keeps flitting to the right, to her side mirror. A black sedan overtakes us on double white lines. I cannot see the driver, but I do see Othilia, half her body through the passenger window. She flips her middle finger at us, laughing as they pass.

"Ryder! It's her," Mishca yells over the engine roar.

"What's going on?" I glance back at Nerissa as she rubs her eyes. Dylan still snores beside her.

"Othilia. She just overtook us." I fiddle with my phone.

"Have you got the direction to Tammy's?" Mishca's grip on the wheel tightens as the car jerks forward.

"Nearly."

"Please, hurry. I can't let this happen again."

"Maybe we should call the police and tell them there's a crime in progress at Tammy's place. That'll get the police there before Othilia," Nerissa says.

"No." Mishca glances at the van's mirrors. "Police will complicate things. Othilia might kill them for starters. But then also Michelle's death will be on their radar soon. We don't need to bring to anyone's attention a bunch of identical looking girls. Besides, they might not even make it there in time. We're not that far away."

Nerissa sighs. I provide directions as we continue

from the outskirts of Townsville through to the inner suburbs. It only takes fifteen minutes, but it feels longer than the rest of the trip combined.

"Turn here." I point right as we pass the signage indicating we have reached the suburb of West End.

She takes another turn, and then I point and call, "There! Number eight."

We stare at the large brick home, surrounded by hibiscus hedges and a quaint arch over a path that leads to the front stairs. The black sedan Othilia rode in is nowhere in sight.

"I don't feel her Ryder. I should be able to feel it if I'm around one of my sisters. There's nothing. We're too late."

"Oh, babe." I reach across and squeeze her arm.

"Wait, Mishca." Nerissa's hushed voice holds a tinge of excitement at her revelation. "You haven't felt her death either. You said you feel it inside, like you're being torn apart. Have you felt that?"

"You're right." She pauses as though she is letting the revelation digest.

Tammy is alive. Othilia may have overtaken us, but she has not won yet. We can still save Mishca's sister.

Nerissa leans forward, her blond head poking between the seats. "So what should we do now?"

"Stake out the joint maybe?" I suggest.

"I think we should go sleuthing for clues." Nerissa motions toward the house. "Tammy mightn't be home, but someone could be. Maybe we can discover where she is?"

Without a word, my girlfriend opens her door.

"Mishca." Nerissa lurches forward and grasps Mishca's shoulder. "You can't go in there. You look just like her. You might freak the people inside. Or what if they think you're her? Could you pull that off?"

"What if Othilia turns up again, like in Airlie?" Mishca asks, not being able to hide the panic in her voice.

"How about me?" I volunteer.

If Othilia shows up, I have already proven I can handle it. Well, I did once before, not that I am sure I could do it again on command. My powers are anything but tested. *And if Fin thinks I am going to try flying like he got Mishca to do.* That broken part inside me from Fin's inability to accept Mishca protests even thinking about my best friend. He will come around. I am sure of it.

"No." Nerissa pokes her head further through. "If her parents are home I don't think they'd appreciate some strange guy knocking on their door. I'll go." She gives the still-sleeping Dylan a loving glance before climbing carefully from the car so as not to wake him.

Mishca purses her lips as though she is thinking of protesting, but when none comes Nerissa takes it as a yes. The van rocks with Nerissa sliding the door closed and causing a snort from the back seat. Dylan pops his head up. He slept through all the other commotion, but the moment his fiancé leaves he wakes up instantly. It is almost like their personal Bluetooth has disconnected.

"Are we here already?" Dylan's voice is still groggy. "Hey, where's Nerissa?"

"Checking on Tammy's place." Mishca's gaze does not leave the house.

"She's what?" Dylan pulls open the door right as Nerissa skips back across the street shaking her head.

"No one's home." Nerissa sounds as disappointed as the downcast expression on Mischa's face.

"What do you think you were doing?" Dylan's jaw is set hard. "Don't you ever go off like that without me again."

"Babe, I'm fine."

"But you could —"

"But nothing," Nerissa cuts off his protests, "You heard what Mishca's been through. What kind of best friend would I be if I didn't help?" She arches an eyebrow.

"A live one." Dylan folds his arms.

Mishca and I grimace at each other. Nothing quite like the awkwardness of watching a couple fight. Not enjoying being the topic of their fight either.

"Hey." Nerissa places a hand on his. "I'll wake you next time, okay?"

"Okay," Dylan concedes, obviously smitten by his girl.

The two of them kiss and make-up...loudly. I keep my gaze skyward and mouth, "Get a room." Mishca smothers a giggle with her hand.

When the two finally come up for air, Dylan announces, "Man, I'm starving."

"Dylan!" Nerissa slaps him on the arm.

"It's okay. Some sustenance would be good for all of us," Mishca says, but something in her voice leaves a buoy of dread bobbing in my stomach.

CHAPTER 15

MISHCA

"CASTLETOWN SHOPPINGWORLD is a few minutes' drive away." Ryder peers at the map on his phone.

I turn on the car and follow his directions. My mind ticks over. Every time I close my eyes I see Michelle and her blood, Othilia and her crazy-ass sneer. I can still hear her words. *I've got other people to kill.* The image of her crumpled on the floor of Andrea's room plagues me. The way she wanted me dead haunts me. She won't stop.

Where would Othilia go? No doubt she knew that Tammy wasn't home. Chances are she was doing recon on the place, or had prepared an ambush. Or maybe one of her goons watched the place as I didn't feel her presence at all. An icy vortex spirals inside me as anxiousness kicks in. How can I possibly beat her to Tammy? She seems to have the advantage in every way. *Breathe. Calm down.* Maybe focusing on Ryder was wrong. I need to be stronger and my love for him weakens my programming.

I put on a cap and some glasses in an attempt to hide my appearance and push those thoughts away. Once inside, Dylan follows his nose and leads us straight to the food court. Luckily, it's late night shopping or we'd be scrounging food from the supermarket.

We eat in silence. I barely taste the food. My whole body is on Othilia alert. Every time a girl with my skin color or hair goes past, I scan them with suspicion. It's to the point where I get some rude glares.

"Boy. That hit the spot." Ryder leans back and rubs his stomach.

"Pfft. Pitiful," Dylan says with a grin. He hops up and heads to a Chinese takeaway shop to get seconds.

"Not up to the challenge?" Nerissa playful teases. It's unsuitable for the situation. I resist the urge to scowl at her.

"That guy has hollow legs. There is no way I would take him on in an eating contest." Ryder's voice is light and playful to match hers. Now I want to thump them both.

"Why do you do that?" Nerissa asks.

"Do what?" Ryder sounds perplexed.

"Talk without contractions?"

Nerissa's caught on. I've noticed it, and even grilled him on it, but ended up putting it down to Ryder's quirkiness, or him being a grammar nerd.

"I use contractions." Ryder's brows pinch together. "Occasionally."

"No, you don't," Dylan interjects, returning with an

overflowing plate of food. "Kinda reminds me of—ouch, Nerissa. That hurt."

"What?" Nerissa bats her eyelashes like she's innocent, but I saw the kick. I can't think about it too long because it hits me at once. I feel it. The tingling starts at my toes. I swear aloud.

"Is it?" Nerissa's eyes widen.

"Othilia. She's here."

I whip my head around, scanning the crowds for my not-so-nice sister. There's no mirror-image of me in sight. I stand up to get a better observation point, circling around.

There. I see her, standing in the middle of the isle, searching as well. Her hands clutch at the hem of her pink dress. Our gaze locks. Her widened eyes match her gaping mouth. Then her face lights up and she runs towards me, her long straight hair flicking behind her.

It's not Othilia. Her hair is different, her face is softer, sweeter, and there's no gotta-kill-my-sister-crazy in her eyes. I brace myself at first, but her radiating happiness urges me to rush to meet her, ignoring the protests of my friends. We embrace like long lost family.

"You found me," she whispers in my ear. "How did you find me? I've been searching for you for so long. I couldn't get anywhere with the adoption agency. But I never gave up." She pushes me back by my shoulders and stares at me with her matching almond eyes. "We even hired a private detective, not that she got far either. But she was sure I have siblings. Lots of them."

I ache inside. We *had* lots of siblings once. Tammy

jumps up and down on the spot, like a kid hyped up on sugar, and squeals. She's totally oblivious to my pain.

"So...you haven't happened to meet any other long lost relatives recently, have you?" I try to glean if she's had any contact from Othilia yet.

She shakes her head. "You're the only one."

Tammy turns and notices my friends. She raises an eyebrow when her gaze hits Ryder.

"Who's the tattooed hottie? Please tell me that's not our brother."

"Ah, definitely not." I guide her closer to my friends and then make the introductions. "This is my boyfriend, Ryder, my best friend, Nerissa, and her boyfriend, Dylan. This is, Tammy, my errr, sister."

The guys nod and my bestie goes in for a hug.

"It's so lovely to meet you." Nerissa disentangles herself from Tammy.

"Hey, I only live a few minutes away. Let's go back there and catch up."

"No," Nerissa, Ryder, and I cry in unison, causing Tammy to take a step back. She knows we're kin, but she has no idea the danger she's in.

"What we mean is we've got a booking at ah, um, resort. It's got a pool and a spa," Nerissa says in her sweet, innocent voice, and then adds in a whisper, "And my dad's paying. We should kick back there instead."

A devious expression spreads across Tammy's face. "Sounds like a plan."

The tingling from Tammy has dissipated. I'm relieved. Now I can be on high alert as we head to the car. I don't sense Othilia at all as we head to the van.

"Can we swing by the house to grab my togs?" Tammy asks. It's an innocent question, but it makes us all cringe.

"It's okay," I answer. "I've got a spare set. Besides, the pool closes at ten. We don't want to waste spa time." I keep my voice light. "Do you need to let your folks know? You could call them?"

"Nah. It's cool. My folks are at a medical conference in Melbourne for a few days."

Ryder drives with Dylan riding shotgun, allowing us girls to pile into the back. Nerissa keeps glancing from my newfound sister to me, her eyes bugging a little. She saw the clones in the goo, but seeing another me breathing the same air as us is another thing altogether.

Tammy clutches my hand and squeezes it. "I can't believe you're here. I've got so many questions."

I feign a laugh. "Let's wait until we get to the resort." The reality is I'm worried she'll bolt if I tell her the truth now. Though really, there's nothing stopping her from running from me at our cabin either.

Slipping off my cap and fake glasses, I examine Tammy. My two run-ins with Othilia gave me little time to take in the other clones properly. It's hard with the intermittent shadows that come when we're not under a streetlight. But each time her face is illuminated I see me staring through her eyes.

We pull up at the tourist park—not a high-end resort that we led Tammy to believe—and Nerissa heads to reception, returning quickly with our key.

Ryder drives to our cabin and we unload the van.

"Why did you girls have to bring so much stuff?" Dylan grumbles at the stuff piled around his legs.

Nerissa and I giggle and ignore him. Ryder gives me a faint grimace. I can't read what he thinks of the whole situation.

"Oh, swanky." Tammy wrinkles her nose as we enter.

It's not. The décor screams the '80s and it's in rough condition.

"The pictures online made it out to be much nicer." Assuming Tammy's programming isn't triggered, she shouldn't catch Nerissa's lie. But the signs are there, easy for me to detect.

Dylan takes his and Nerissa's bags into the bedroom while Ryder leaves ours next to the double bed in the common area. Severe lack of privacy, but it was the only room they had that would fit us all.

Tammy jumps onto the bed. She's so excited. My mouth sets downwards. I'm going to have to burst her bubble pretty soon. Thoughts of Michelle make it hard.

"So, come on, spill. How did you manage to get through the agency cone of silence?" Tammy giggles as she asks.

"I had hacker help." Without Connor's skills I'd be none the wiser. "But there's more to it than that."

Tammy cocks her head, but stays silent. All eyes in the room are on her.

I fold my arms and take a sudden interest in the ground. "What are your views on IVF?"

"I dunno." Tammy stares at me blankly at first.

"Are we, like, IVF babies? You know how that chick had those octuplets." She seems more enthused.

"Kind of." I chew on my thumbnail again. "But you understand the science behind it?"

"Sort of. Biology was never one of my best subjects." She gives me a sheepish grin.

"I sucked at it too." That's the first thing that we've found in common. I'm sure there will be more.

It's time. I take a deep breath. "We were experimental b-births. We were genetically engineered through a cell duplication process." I'm not even sure if what I'm saying is the exact science, but I want to soften the blow.

"So, we're special." Tammy breaks into a wide grin. It feels so weird to be watching my face on someone else go through these emotions.

"You could say that." I ignore Dylan's sarcasm laced words, but his fiancé doesn't. She elbows him hard enough to produce a "hey."

"Definitely special." I pause for a moment. "So, do you understand how we were created?" I say the right term. There's no going back now.

"Not really. But I get the general gist of it. So, we —" The light bulb goes off for Tammy. "Are you serious?"

I nod. "I've managed to get some documents, if you want to see them."

Tammy sits still on the bed with a dazed expression on her face. "Wait. I'm a clone?" She holds my gaze in awkward contemplation. "You're a clone? Like that sheep?"

"Yes," I whisper.

"Shut. Up." She gets up and pushes me in the chest, though her shove doesn't even budge me. She hasn't been activated.

"Do you guys want to wait outside for a moment?" I feel comfortable enough to be alone with Tammy, especially now I know she's weaker than me.

"Okay. But we will be outside the door." Ryder waves at the exit. "Right outside."

"No, it's fine. Go grab something from the caravan shop for dessert," I insist. The last thing my sister needs is to be under the microscope with the others staring at her like some science experiment, even if we are one.

We both stay silent until the others have left.

"So are we the same person?" Tammy asks, a bit more nervous now.

My eyes follow her as she paces up and down the room. "No. We're definitely individuals, but we come from the same, err, base subject — err, donor."

"Wow." Her face goes blank, devoid of any emotion. "As a little girl I always dreamed I was special, someone different. That my parents were famous rock stars who gave me up before they made it big. But I never could have imagined something like this."

"I know. It's the last thing I expected when we broke into EEFS." I sit on the bed now that I'm convinced Tammy isn't freaked enough to do a runner.

"This is starting to make sense. I was constantly mistaken for this chick called Michelle. How many of us are there?" Tammy's voice sounds distant and cut off. She may be in shock.

The mention of Michelle hollows me. I see her, laying on the floor, the color draining from her face, her lifeless eyes staring at nothing. Squeezing my eyelids shut, I will the image away and take a deep breath.

"There were thirty of us," I manage to whisper.

"Were?" There's an edge of urgency to her voice. "How many are left now?"

"Four— I mean three." My voice cracks, but I remain composed. "Most died from our weak hearts." I pull down the neckline of my shirt to reveal my scar. "I had a heart transplant last year."

Tammy's face is streaked with tear tracks. She pulls hers down to reveal a much fainter scar. "My parents found out about my heart condition when I was a tween. We were living in Europe at the time. They managed to find a donor for me a couple of years later."

That explains why there was no record of whether Tammy had been "repaired" or not.

"You said *most*. What happened to the others?"

"That's why I'm here." I ball my hands into fists and take a sharp breath. "You're in danger. One of our sisters is in town. She's been sent to kill you."

CHAPTER 16

RYDER

"HEY, DYLAN," I SAY tentatively. "Remember at the shopping center you said the way I talked reminded you of someone. I wanted to ask you more about that."

He shifts uncomfortably as Nerissa glares at him. "It was some family acquaintances who visited my parents from the old country. They would come by every few years as we grew up. They moved away, but their kids live here now."

"Dylan." Nerissa's fingertips go to her lips as though she can stop him from blurting out more.

"Babe, he has a right to know. You've seen what Mishca went through."

"We don't even know if he is related to them. He's meeting his mum when we get back. Just drop it." Her voice is harder than I have ever heard it before.

"I have actually already met my mum, well the woman who gave me up for adoption. It only gave me more questions. Sophitia told Mishca she is my cousin. If you will not help, maybe she will." The energy pulses through me, wanting free of my skin. I breathe deeply, willing it back inside.

"Ryder," Nerissa's voice softens. "It's not that I don't care. I have family obligations, secrets to protect. I'm going against my parents' wishes by telling you anything." She glances at her fiancé, and then back to me. "Please, don't tell Mishca. In this circumstance, family has to come above all else. Talk to Sophitia and you'll understand because I think Dylan may be right. But it's not our place to say."

I can feel my tattoos tingling and a rising urge to make Nerissa talk. In an instant, I envision my hands around her neck with blue bolts sparking to loosen her tongue.

"No!" My fists clench tight as I will the thoughts away.

"What do you mean 'no'?" Dylan takes a step forward to put himself between me and Nerissa.

"Nothing." I did not realize I had spoken aloud. "I understand your family loyalty and will not disrespect that."

"We're going to go down to the store." Nerissa gestures towards the front entrance. "Are you going to come?"

"No, I will wait here."

"Do you want us to get you something?"

"Surprise me."

I lean up against our cabin, tormented by the fact that the truth is so close and yet so far away. The pieces of the puzzle do not fit together. There is a chance that I am some distant relative of people who are friends with Dylan's family, that I am Sophitia's relative, and then there was that guy who was talking about a friend of Sophitia's, which could have been me. Not that I have ever seen them spark blue.

My eyelids slide shut. Everything goes swirling through my mind. I try to focus on something, anything that will make me feel more in control. Something to keep me grounded. Without warning, my mind reels back and throws me into a memory not forgotten, but not fully remembered until now.

Mist hangs in the air as my mother races down an alley. Her breath is short and sharp. Each step jostles me in her arms.

"My Lady, are you sure about this?" comes a voice beside me.

"Yes, I am. If my son is to stand a chance, he must be hidden from Wirth. That monster has already stolen so much from our people. He is our last hope, but he must reach maturity. If his powers are not able to fully develop, then he will never be the savior we need."

I snuggle closer to my mother's breasts at her words.

"But how will he survive? He cannot fend for himself yet."

"Commander, you know what I must do."

My subconscious battles to keep my own memories from me and I lose the scene for a moment. Then, it comes back and it is the very memory I have held onto for years.

My mother reaches down and puts me in a crib, her long wispy blond hair falling onto my face. I stare up at her pale cheeks, reaching for her with my chubby baby fists.

"My darling child," her lips are like pink rose petals in the morning dew, "it is time for you to go and join your new family. They can give you what I cannot, shelter and protection. But you must change to be accepted with them. Do not be like me. Be like them and you will be fine. Be Ryder."

A single crystal tear rolls down each of her blue eyes, slides over her cheeks, and falls onto my face. She kisses me and goes. I cry for her to not leave me. I cry so hard it feels like this sorrow will never end. But I obey her. I change. And in the distance, another baby cries.

My lids snap open. Another baby. That part of the memory is new. And Wirth! He has something to do with my mother abandoning me. There is nothing I can do to stop the build-up of charge inside as my anger surges forward. I grit my teeth to stifle a yell, clap my hands together and point them at a nearby palm tree. The blue electricity shoots from me, disintegrating the tree to a pile of ash.

I stare at my hands, fearing Mishca may be right after all. I am a weapon of Wirth's, like her.

CHAPTER 17

MISHCA

"WHAT DO YOU MEAN she's been sent to kill me?" Tammy's mouth hangs agape.

"Othilia isn't like us," I pause, searching for the words to explain this. "She's evil. I think our creator, Wirth, raised her. She's been sent to kill any of the clones from her batch that are 'defective.'" I use air-quotes.

"That's crazy," she exclaims. "You can't go around killing people."

It obviously still hasn't sunk in that her perception of reality doesn't equate to the world we've been thrust into.

"She's already killed Michelle Cooper." I can't keep the sadness from my voice.

"No." She sinks onto the bed beside me and clutches the pillow, pulling it to her like a puffy security blanket.

"I was there, in Mackay." I hang my head. "I tried so hard to save her, but I underestimated Othilia.

There's no way I'm going to let her get you."

"And she's here now?"

I nod. "She passed us on the way into town. It's pure luck that you weren't home and I got to you first."

Tears prick her eyes and she hugs the pillow tighter. "How did she kill Michelle?"

I tell her in the least graphic way I can. It must have sunk in that our sister is dead. She lets go of her pillow shield and weeps in my arms.

"Shhh, it doesn't matter now. What matters is I found you, and Andrea is safe in Europe for now." She actually could be safe there anyway, given that Wirth didn't know Tammy got a transplant there. All I can do is pray she's too far away for them to get to her.

"I'm glad you didn't kill her. We can't be like her." I help her wipe away her tears. Then, the questions begin. "How did you find out all this?"

I give her the basic rundown—my nightmares, the fake adoption agency, the cloning facility, how we found her, Michelle, and Andrea. She listens intently, at times dragging her hand over her face to remove any trace of tears.

"So you have bad dreams every night?" Tammy screws up her nose. Her eyes are still tinged with red.

"Yeah." I sigh, thinking how I'm going to have to endure another one in a few hours. That is if I can actually get some sleep. "They always have this guy in them too. I'm thinking it must be Wirth, the guy who created us. At least that's what's in the files we stole."

"I don't know how you're still sane, putting up with those dreams for the last few months."

"Now that I know what they are, they've lost their impact a bit. Have you had anything like that?" I ask her.

"No." She fiddles with the hem of her shirt. "I barely remember my dreams, and when I do, they're rarely nightmares." She's still normal, for now.

"That's a good thing in one way. It means you haven't been called for duty." Despite the relief at this news, anger bubbles inside. Why me? Why did I get activated and not Tammy? We both had the same operation.

Tammy bites her bottom lip. "I hadn't given it that much thought. I just figured we were an experiment. You know, someone proving that they could clone a human."

"I wish it was that simple." My hands involuntarily form fists as though they're readying to smash our maker in the face for the pain he's caused. "This wasn't ego. It appears to be war."

"War?" Fear clouds my sister's eyes.

"We're meant to be sleeper soldiers. Kinda like spies. The plan seemed to be to create us, farm us out through a fake adoption agency, and then activate us at the right time. The file specified that we are designer soldiers, but it never said who we were made to fight."

To be honest, I hadn't given the whole "soldier" concept much thought. I still can't fathom that I'd been created with the singular purpose of fighting some unknown enemy. My focus has been on saving my sisters. A blur of war images flashes through my mind. It's not somewhere I want to be. I shudder.

"So your dreams are linked to that?" Tammy crosses her legs and rests on the edge of the bed.

I nod. "They're meant to be a form of mind control, making my will weaker and my thoughts more open to suggestion." I shrug. "It doesn't seem to be working so well. It might be because my programming wasn't triggered intentionally. I think it's faulty."

"So that's it. You get activated, you get bad dreams?" Tammy's brows rise.

"Not quite." I release my fingers from their tight ball and flex them on my thighs. "I also have, ah, enhancements." For some reason Tammy gawps at my breasts. I laugh. "Not those type of enhancements."

I walk to the kitchen cupboards and pull a cast iron frying pan from a shelf. Holding it up so she can see, I place my hands on either side and fold it in half like I am doing origami.

"Whoa." Tammy's mouth hangs open.

"I'm fast too."

"So do you remember being activated at all? Did you wake up one morning and you were stronger, faster, and having nightmares?" She flops back onto the bed, staring up at the ceiling. Her mouth pinches into a straight line.

"I think my heart transplant triggered it. I'm not sure if it was intentional or not, but the dreams started straight after surgery. There's meant to be a reprogramming process, but as far as I can tell that hasn't fully happened to me yet." I stand up and lean against the bedroom wall with my arms folded.

"How could they do this to us?" Tammy whispers.

"Well, there's a chip in our brains—"

Tammy bolts into a sitting position. "There's a what in our brains?"

"A chip. It delivers the compliance program and triggers the genetically modified enhancements." My voice sounds detached. I've gone through this in my head so many times, it doesn't get to me anymore. I've accepted it as fact. "That's why they want to kill you. The chip is proof that we've been tampered with."

"But they don't want to kill you, right?" Tammy chews on her thumbnail.

"Well, Othilia would. But no, as far as I can tell our creator wants me alive, for now at least. It appears our original had a condition they weren't aware of until after the process. They know I've been repaired, so I'm fit for duty because of my recent heart transplant. But they still think you're defective. They don't know you've had a heart transplant." I let free a rueful laugh. "They're worried an autopsy would reveal our uniqueness. According to their calculations, you and Andrea are past your expiration dates. Can't have dead clones with chips in their brains lying around waiting for an autopsy."

Tammy stares off through the window as though she's lost in thought. I can't blame her. It's a lot to take in. She sweeps some stray hair from her cheek and tucks it behind her ear. I wonder how long it took for her to grow it and then straighten it. Mine never seems to get that long with my springy curls.

Without the difference in hairdo, we'd be identical. There are no subtle differences like there was with

Othilia. Mind you, *she'd* still pass for me in most situations. There's no way I could blame anyone for getting Othilia and I mixed up.

"How did you manage to get your hair that long and so straight?" My thoughts spill from my mouth. I can't stand silence for too long, and girl stuff is my default setting.

"What?" Tammy jerks toward me. Her face is still emanating the whole dazed and confused vibe. "Oh, my hair? Extensions— insta-hair! I had to beg my parents for—" At the mention of her parents, Tammy's eyes go wide, filled with fear. "Mishca! What about my parents? Will the assassin come for them too?"

Nausea washes over me. There's a chance that Othilia would be happy with some collateral damage. Especially given she's only gotten one of the three kills she wanted.

"Unknown," I whisper. "It's possible." I stop talking. It hurts too much to see the pain in her eyes.

"What are we going to do?"

I suck on my lip and think. "You can't stay here but you sure can't go home. She'll find you and kill you. Othilia is stronger than me too. I won't be able to protect you. We need to be smarter than her."

Tammy wrings her hands together, breathing sharply.

"Don't worry, we'll think of something." I find that soothing tone that my mum used on me when I was young and in the throes of what we thought was a panic attack.

It's not like we have a uni-mind, but there's

definitely a connection. Tammy seems to calm with my words.

"Come on, let's go get an ice cream." I don't want to leave her alone. "If we sit here and dwell on this all day, we'll drive ourselves crazy."

She nods and heads for the door. As I step outside the cabin my soldier sense prickles and a figure moves to my left. Instinctively, I twist and throw a punch, knocking the intruder to the ground.

CHAPTER 18

RYDER

I LOSE CONTROL OF THE ENERGY inside me as I land on the ground. A blue bolt springs from my hands into the grounds as I brace for impact, lighting up the area around us. Pain shoots through my chest where Mishca's fist connected.

"Are you okay?" Mishca kneels beside me while I struggle for breath.

Tammy stands behind her, open-mouthed.

"Oh, I'm so sorry."

"You punch harder than Dylan." I grimace, still clutching my chest. "I guess we know who wears the pants in this relationship."

I expect her to flinch at that, but she beams at me instead. She has been all hot and cold since Mackay. Almost a repeat of when Colin came on the scene. She kept distancing herself from me then, and now it is like she wants to slip through my fingers again. Maybe she regrets not trusting him with her secret and not giving it a go with him. Or maybe she is worried I will be a distraction to her quest to save her sisters. Michelle did die the day we got back together.

"What was that?" Tammy asks, staring at me.

Mishca ignores her and reaches a hand, helping me to my feet. "What were you doing hanging around the door like that?"

"I needed some time alone." I glance at the pile of ash that was once a tree.

Mishca's gaze follows mine. "Did you do that?"

I nod.

"Wait," Tammy says, squeaking like a mouse. "You can do some weird stuff with fire? Was that fire? Or electricity? Are you a clone too? Can you do stuff with fire, Mishca? Do we have super freaky powers?"

Mishca raises her hands and then fans them up and down in a calm-it motion. "We don't know what Ryder is, but we don't think he is like us."

"I remember my mother giving me up," I say, recalling the resurfaced memory that resulted in my uncontrolled sparkage. I turn to Mishca. "More came back to me just a few minutes ago about Mum. When she gave me up there was another baby there. And she mentioned hiding me from Wirth."

Mishca inhales sharply. After glancing sideways at her sister, she gives me the this-is-not-the-time signal with her eyes. "We'll talk more later."

Tammy opens her mouth as though she is going to protest but then presses her lips together without saying a word.

Soldier-Mishca emerges and puts a finger to her lips to tell us to be quiet and signals for me to get behind

Tammy. I get into position and peer around, but cannot see anything to cause alarm. Closing my eyes, I make an effort to focus my hearing like Mishca can. I hear nothing but the sound of cars driving past and waves lapping against the sand from the beach across the road. After a few steps, she stops, foot hovering in the air with her fingers and signing stuff I do not understand.

Tammy bumps into her. "Oi. What's going on, sis?"

The family reference appears to snap Mishca back. "I needed to make sure we were in a secure location because I know what we need to do." The excitement in her voice overrides the military tone and she sounds like herself again.

I cock my head to the side, imagining scenarios of what the heck she has in mind.

"Come on. We need to talk to the others." She turns around and sprints to the shop.

Nerissa and Dylan sit at a table, each with an ice cream in hand, noticeably without the other desserts they were meant to be getting.

"Are you okay?" Nerissa asks Tammy.

"As well as can be expected." She tries to sound casual, but there is an edge to her voice.

She breaks eye contact with Nerissa. Everything around us appears peaceful and tranquil, nothing like the atmosphere between us, which is as charged as my hands were when I shot electricity at Othilia. I really need to talk to Sophitia.

"So what are we going to do now?" Dylan asks and then takes a long lick of his ice cream.

Mishca turns with a maniacal smile plastered across her face. "We're going to kidnap Tammy."

"Wait. What? Kidnap Tammy?" I cannot determine a scenario where that will make things better.

Dylan scratches his head. "I don't get it."

Mishca faces each of us in turn, looking more military-like than I have ever seen her before. Something in the way she stands, so rigid and commanding. "It's simple. If she stays here, she'll be in danger. If we hide Tammy, her parents will be in danger. But if we fake a kidnapping, there'll be media attention. It will send a clear message that she's not at her house and that her parents don't know where she is. That will keep them safe."

A fake grin spreads across my face. "Perfect. We can stash Tammy at my place until we determine our next course of action." There is actually a chance that Othilia will still go for her parents and hold them hostage, suspecting that we have had a hand in Tammy's disappearance. Or she could just kill them in a fit of pique. I would not put anything past her. But this is still the best option we have.

"How long will that be?" Nerissa asks.

"I have no idea." Mishca shrugs, but does not stop surveying the area. "At the moment, I'm scanning for immediate threats. We can figure a better plan once Tammy is safe."

"But my parents," Tammy says, her voice tight with concern. My stomach tightens. *Has she read my mind?* "They'll be so worried."

I exhale, making an effort not to show I was holding

my breath.

"Better that they're worried than dead." Nerissa is practical, though her voice is kind and soothing. "If you want to keep them safe, I think this is the best option."

Tammy sits on a bench, staring off. Her body tenses as she bites her lip. At last, she lifts her head. "You're right. I can't think of any other alternative."

Mishca sits beside her and puts her hand on her sister's shoulder in a reassuring gesture. She does not pull it off.

"So how are we going to get Tammy back to Brisbane without Othilia finding out?" I lean against the wall with my arms folded, my brow pinched.

"Chances are Othilia and her associates will be watching the airports, bus stations, and car rentals," Nerissa offers. "I'm sure if we book anything in Mishca's name it will get back to them."

"Then you book it in my name," Dylan says. I resist the urge to give him a fist bump. "I've got the most separation from Mishca. They might have researched her best friend and her boyfriend, but I doubt they've gone to the trouble to find who her best friend's boyfriend is. Mishca and Ryder take their flights back as planned so not as to arouse suspicion while Nerissa and I drive Tammy back to Brisbane in the van."

Nerissa gives Dylan a huge hug. "That's perfect."

One look at Mishca and I know she does not agree.

CHAPTER 19

MISHCA

I SUCK ON MY BOTTOM LIP. The thought of being separated from my sister terrifies me. I want to be with her to protect her. But that could put her in more danger. Part of me wants to stop this now. Knowing it's our best option is the only thing keeping my mouth shut.

"Let's go back to the cabin and put together a plan," Tammy says.

The five of us walk down the stairs. Dylan and Nerissa whisper to each other, though I can still hear them. They are mainly talking through different options to keep everyone safe. I block them out and run scenarios over in my head to determine what we need to do. Ryder opens the door and everyone but Nerissa heads for the dining room table.

Nerissa goes into her bedroom in search of a notebook. I can hear her rummaging through her bags until finally returning with pen and paper in hand. We throw around all types of ideas for the best way to fake a kidnapping.

"I thought we could make it appear like a break in, but going back to Tammy's house is not an option." Dylan rubs his chin like he's *The Thinker* transformed from bronze to flesh. "If they see her, she's dead. If they see Mishca, they'll follow her. And if they see Ryder, Nerissa, or me, we'll be on their radar."

"How do we know I'm not already on their radar?" Nerissa asks. She closes her eyes for a moment. "I've already been to Tammy's house. They would have seen that I came from the same van Mishca was driving up here. A unicorn emblazoned van kind of makes a statement."

For one horrible moment, I think Nerissa might be right and I screw my eyes up in frustration. Then, I remember.

"I never felt Othilia there." I try to sound reassuring. Dylan reaches over and gives Nerissa's hand a squeeze.

"They seemed to have pretty thorough files on the clone clan," I continue. "So I would guess that with you not being home, they were prepared to search for you somewhere else you might regularly go. Chances are they're still here." I'm grasping at straws, but there's a chance it's true. "But you definitely need to get a different van. Someone else might have the house under surveillance. Go through a different company to be safe."

Tammy taps her fingers on the table. "It's going to be hard to fake my kidnapping without any hard evidence."

We all go quiet. I can't extract the image of Michelle from my head. Tammy mustn't die. I have to find a solution.

I have the answer. "A frantic phone call from Tammy would do it."

"What do you mean?" Nerissa face scrunches.

"Tammy calls triple zero and says she thinks someone is following her and that she is in danger. Put on a bit of acting, pretend like someone snatches you while on the call. She dumps the phone after they drive off."

"That could work." Ryder sounds as optimistic as I feel.

"You'll need a disguise." I reach forward and lift a lock of her hair. "We don't want Nerissa and Dylan to wind up kidnapping suspects. When we leave here tomorrow, you need to look like someone else."

"Did you class what you had on when we met as a disguise?" Tammy smirks. "No offence, but it was pretty lame."

"Does that mean I get to go shopping?" Nerissa claps her hands together in excitement. Dylan groans.

"Yes, it does," I say, unable to stop from grinning. "Tammy will need a wig and some clothes that cover her up."

"I always wondered what I'd be like as a blond." Tammy flicks her hair over her shoulder.

"What about Andrea?" Ryder asks. "We need to warn her."

"I'm not sure yet." I run my thumb over my bottom lip. "I'll have to think on it some more."

We talk some finer details over the next hour. As the time drags on, the conversation slows.

"Bedtime I think." Ryder yawns. He pushes his chair from the table and then moves over to the lounge.

"You're sleeping there?" I ask, unable to disguise my disappointment. His arms act as my security blanket, and after what I've been through, I need a little TLC.

"I thought you would want to have Tammy close. You know, in case Othilia has somehow managed to track us down."

He's right. Besides, how can you rip someone from their normal life and then expect them to sleep on a lounge?

"Sure." I don't let my sad-sackness take me over with Tammy a few meters away.

Ryder pulls me to him and gives me a hug. "It will all be okay. Get some sleep. It is going to be a big day tomorrow." He lies down, hidden from sight by the back of his makeshift bed.

"Night everyone," Nerissa calls.

"Don't have too much fun with the ladies." Dylan hoots. "Double the fun."

"Huh?" Tammy cocks her head.

"Ewww, Dylan. You do realize Tammy and I share the same DNA." I throw a cushion at his head and hit him flush in the face.

"Dude—" Ryder takes a step forward, but I place my hand on his chest to stop him right as the verbal berating starts from Nerissa.

"Sorry, babe. It was meant to be a joke." Dylan

glances at me. "Sorry, Mishca, Tammy, Ryder. That was rude." He keeps a straight face, but the corners of his mouth twitch.

Asshat.

"Honestly, you are so immature sometimes." Nerissa huffs. "Let's try this again. Goodnight."

"Sweet dreams." Dylan lets a smirk dance across his face before closing their bedroom door.

Yeah, right. I snatch up a T-shirt and a pair of shorts and hand them to Tammy. "These should be okay to sleep in."

"Thanks." Tammy hugs them to her chest. Her eyes droop and convey sadness. I've been there. I understand the depression she can easily fall into from here.

Turning around to give her some privacy, I take off my own clothes and change into my boxer shorts and pajama top. Tammy turns off the light and we get into bed.

"I'm glad you found me," she whispers in the dark.

"Me too," I say, and mean it.

My eyes feel heavy, but I resist closing them because every time I do I see Michelle's lifeless body. But I can't fight off the tiredness for long and am pulled into sleep.

"Mishca."

My own voice calls from the darkness. I walk down a corridor that appears to have no end. I peek behind me. I can't see where the corridor begins either. Even though there are no windows, a cool breeze tickles my skin, causing me to shiver.

"Mishca. Save me."

I walk faster towards the voice, spurred on by a sense of urgency.

"You can't save them all," a male voice says.

I glance over my shoulder and see the silhouette of a man with long brown hair. Wirth.

"You can only save yourself. Come to me."

My feet break into a run.

"Mishca. Help me."

A door appears up ahead on my left. My sister's voice seems to be coming from inside. I cast a glimpse back down the corridor towards Wirth before yanking the door open.

"Mishca. Save me."

A mass of Imogene clones lay in a pile on the floor with their throats slit. Eyes like mine stare back vacantly. Something touches my foot. I squeal and jerk my foot away.

It's Tammy, crawling to me. Her hair is matted with blood. Red dribbles from her mouth as she opens it to speak. "You promised you'd keep me safe." Maggots spill from the wound in her throat. "You lied."

The mound of clones that were still on the ground jerk up to sitting positions and crawl towards me.

I turn to flee but run into a closed door. Grappling with the door handle, I strain and rattle it, but it won't budge. The super human strength that broke off the hospital handle fails me.

"You lied," the horde says in unison. "You killed us all."

My eyes fly open and I'm in our motel room again. Even through closed doors, I can hear Dylan's snores and it's strangely reassuring.

I reach over to Tammy, who is asleep on her side with her

back to me, and shake her gently. "Tammy, you awake?"

There's no response. Panicking, I roll her over to me.

A large knife protrudes from her stomach. Her dead eyes stare back at me.

I scream.

"Mishca! Wake up," Tammy pleads.

My eyes spring open and I suck in air to calm my racing heart. My sister pounces on me with a smothering embrace.

Ryder bolts up. "Is everyone okay?"

Disentangling myself from Tammy, I give Ryder a nod. "I'll be fine. It was one of the usual ones."

"Are you sure?" Ryder's eyes fill with concern.

I manage another nod.

"Do you want a drink of water?" Tammy hovers over me, just like Mum used to when I had my weak heart.

"That'd be great." I run my tongue over my lips to moisten them.

"I can sleep on the floor next to you if you want," Ryder says after Tammy has left the room.

"No, don't be silly. I should be alright now." I check my watch. 2:30 a.m.

Tammy returns with the water. After drinking half of it, I place the glass on the bedside table.

"Okay. I guess I will head back to the couch." He leans in and kisses me on the cheek. I resist the urge to clutch him to me and squish him until the bad goes away. But I keep my hands by my side.

I watch him leave and then lie back down. Tammy's head hits her pillow at the same time as mine.

"That sounded bad." Tammy's voice quavers. "Was that one of those dreams?"

"Yeah." I don't want to meet her eyes. "Not anything you have to worry about."

"Yet," Tammy whispers in the dark.

CHAPTER 20

RYDER

I STARE AT THE CEILING wishing slumber still held me. Mishca dominated my dreams until a spasm in my calf woke me. I ache all over from my cramped sleeping space. The clock on the microwave reads 5:00 a.m. The sunrise would make a better view than the mold spots I have been counting for the last thirty minutes like sheep.

Swinging my feet around, I stand and stretch, letting my joints find relief in a chorus of cracks. I glance at Mishca in case her super hearing also works when she is sleeping. But she lays motionless, like someone under anaesthetic waiting for an operation.

Is that how she was when she had her transplant?

I shudder as images of Mishca split open, technically dead on the operating table, flash through my mind. I had never thought of her like that before, even though I knew she had her heart removed and someone else's put in her. Man, this is the last thing I want to think about. I let my thoughts wander to Rosie, trying to fathom how she could be the one who gave me up for adoption but not the mother I remember. It does not make any sense at all.

My chest tightens and the walls seem to close in. The desire for fresh air grips me. I have to escape. I tread lightly towards the glass sliding door. My fingers find the lock and I grip it, sliding it into the unlock position. Each time the door screeches in protest I flinch. Flicking the curtain aside, I step out, and secure the room again with the key.

The early morning sky is a still dark blue curtain embossed with silver stars. To the east there is only a hint of sunrise, a small soft lavender glow on the horizon. The water across the road calls to me. I inhale deeply, letting the salty air expand my lungs. Slipping on my flip-flops, I stroll to the front of the park and across the road to the beach.

Kicking off my shoes, my feet sink into the cool sand. Too many thoughts swirl through my mind. My morphing powers, my non-mother, Sophitia, Mishca and her sisters. I turn left and walk up the beach, willing my mind to empty. I lose track of time as I go, my only company being the occasional early riser who jogs or rides past on the path that divides the beach and the road.

Each time my inner turmoil becomes too much, the hairs on my arms rise and my tattoos begins to shimmer. It is almost like the more I use my energy, the more it wants to break free and play, whether I want it to or not. When it gets to the point that I might lose control I stop and beat it back with some yoga. A bit of downward dog, cobra, and warrior pose seems to do the trick. The only thought I let bounce around in my head is my love for Mishca. My skin stops humming and I stare at the water.

The surface gleams invitingly as the sun battles off the night. I had not even noticed until now that the sky had been taken over by the dawn. I stroll right to the water's edge and let the night-chilled waves lap against my toes. Goosebumps ripple over my body.

"Isn't that freezing?" Mishca's warm breath tickles my ear.

My whole body jolts, but I manage to keep my mini lightning bolts under my skin.

"You should not sneak up on people like that." I let my lungs expand with much-needed oxygen.

"Unless you're practicing your tracking skills. And by the way, you could use some stealth lessons. Could you have been any noisier when you left?"

"I thought you were still asleep, that your super soldier mode was taking a break."

Mishca's lips purse together and then twitch from side to side. "My senses don't get down times. And I decided to let you think I was asleep and give you a thirty-minute head start."

"How could you track me across the road?" I have only ever seen Mishca track someone through bushland, not in an urban environment.

"I could hear your energy. You must have been getting a bit worked up over something."

"Great. I am not going to start attracting dogs, am I?"

She chuckles. "Wrong frequency I think. When your energy lets loose it's like these low soundwaves pulse from you. And today you were giving off this weird heat signature."

"Is that like Predator vision?"

"Gee thanks. Way to make a girl feel attractive. Compare her to a grotesque Schwarzenegger-hunting alien." She rolls her eyes.

"Not exactly my desired outcome. But you know what I mean. I am trying to get an understanding of where things are for you. Do you think you are still developing more powers?"

She shrugs. "I don't know. I haven't experienced that one before. What were you doing when you stopped?"

"You could tell I stopped?"

"Yep."

"I was doing yoga, and thinking of you." I step to Mishca and slide my arms around her waist.

"So instead of Predator vision, it's a love connection, maybe?" Her teeth gleam at me as she laughs. Then she snakes her hands through my hair and pulls me to her. Our lips connect and all my worries slip away quicker than during any yoga session.

CHAPTER 21

MISHCA

NERISSA SURE WENT TO town on Tammy. Wig, colored contacts, and male clothes transform Tammy from Mishca look-a-like to skater dude. Her outfit is nice and baggy to hide her curves. Nerissa and I bound her chest as well to be safe. Tammy cried when we cut off her extensions to get her hair to fit under the wig. Thanks to Townsville's theatre community, Nerissa also found some quality stage makeup to camouflage Tammy's skin. Now my sister and I are barely alike at first glance. The facial features are still the same, but the changes should be enough.

It's so strange to see her appear so different. If I didn't know it was Tammy and passed her like this on the street, I would think she was a guy falling on the androgynous side. Nerissa and Dylan are also incognito, just in case they are spotted, but their changes aren't as dramatic—a wig, cap, and some sunglasses.

The now-brunette Nerissa and I sit with Tammy—

aka Tony — on the bench, tucked away at the back of a park in the shadows.

Ryder works a key off his keyring and tosses it to Tammy. "You better take this. You should be right to bunk at my place by yourself until we get back into town. But stay invisible."

"And you need to remain a dude until you get to Brisbane." I ignore the protests my churning stomach makes at the thought of being separated from my sister. "But even then you'll have to be in disguise whenever you leave the house."

"I have heaps of food in the freezer. No one should be coming around while I am away." Ryder plays with a dead leaf.

Thanks to me, we don't need to deal with Fin.

"I'm worried. What if they have your place under observation?" Nerissa clasps a clump of her hair and squeezes it in a small fist. "If Othilia isn't fooled, she might get surveillance at multiple locations, and if she gets Tammy at your place, she could frame you both for her murder."

"Then, we have to make sure Othilia believes we do not know where she is. A drive by should do it. Mishca can make sure she feels Othilia and put on a good show."

We all nod. Time to put those closet acting skills to use.

"Okay, are you ready?" I ask Tammy, fighting the urge to do a third perimeter sweep of the park. I haven't felt Othilia so far, but that doesn't mean we're not in danger.

She nods, the hair on her short brown wig flopping around her now pale face. She could pass for a white guy.

Tammy makes sure no one else is around and then taps in the emergency number. She puts on one of the best acts I've ever heard.

"I need the police." She reaches for her non-existent long hair, her hand finding the back of her neck instead. "My name is Tammy Kanter. Someone's been following me. They tried to push me into a car. I'm scared they're going to—Oh no!" Her voice rises with pretend panic. "They've found me. Please don't. Leave me alone." She actually moves like she is in a struggle and makes grunting noises. "Someone help."

She drops her phone onto the grass, reaches down, and hits the mute button.

"We shouldn't hang around any longer." Dylan pulls his cap down further so his eyes are barely visible. "The police should be able to track that call."

Tammy stands up too. We hug. My arms don't want to let go.

"You take care of yourself," I whisper into her ear.

"You too." She gives me a little squeeze.

"Everything will be okay," Nerissa says, putting on her best reassuring voice. "We'll see you in a couple of days."

I watch the three of them pile into the new hire van with Tammy sitting in the back. We maintain eye contact for as long as we can. I want to keep staring in their direction long after the van has disappeared from view, but there isn't time. The police could be here any minute.

Ryder and I stroll off, hand-in-hand, like two lovers going for a morning walk rather than two culprits leaving the scene of a crime. After a couple of blocks, he stops and pulls me to him, wrapping his arms around my waist. We stay locked together like that until I hear the sirens. I don't want to see the police swarming the park where I said goodbye to Tammy so I break away and head towards Castletown. Ryder catches up in a few strides.

"You going to be okay?"

"As okay as someone can be in this situation." I don't want to sound bitter but fail.

He caresses my hand in his and brings it to his lips for a feather-light kiss. "It is going to be fine. Dylan will take care of them both."

I nod, but I know Dylan isn't enough against Othilia. If only Tammy's heart transplant had activated her too. Then she wouldn't be like a gazelle in the sights of a very hungry lion.

We walk in silence until we reach the shopping center car park and our unicorn emblazed van.

"So you never did tell me what the go was with Dylan punching you." An emptiness sits in my chest that I can't ignore. I bite my lip and force myself to meet Ryder's gaze, not the empty road.

"It was weird. We were at the aqua park, but the two of them stayed away from the water. I decided to have some fun and picked Nerissa up to throw her in and she freaked. Dylan freaked even more and punched me in the jaw. Is Nerissa afraid of water?"

"Not that I know of." I tap my finger against my lips.

My mind ticks over and I realize I've never seen her swimming. She was always off to the side during swimming at school, some medical note getting her out of class. I figure she never wanted to get her perfect hair wet. Nerissa never went for a swim at my place either. Or at the natural lagoon at her parent's house.

"Dylan is super protective of her." Ryder leans against the van and rubs his jaw. "I discovered that the hard way."

I lapse into silence. I'm having trouble concentrating on Ryder's run-in with Dylan and Nerissa as my mind keeps wandering. The fruitless thought, if only Tammy had been activated, repeats like a mantra. Not only would she have the super soldier training, but she wouldn't be in their sights for elimination. Then again, they'd still want her, like they want me. And if she had been activated, she might have been a psycho like Othilia.

"We should drive past her place every day until it appears on the news. Make sure we are seen by your evil twin," Ryder says as though he is reading my thoughts.

"You mean make myself seen. You can be in the back of the van then."

Ryder's eyebrows pinch together. "Chances are they already know about me, babe. You said yourself Othilia has been watching you at home. She would have seen us together at some point. And the way Wirth spoke to me at the club. It was like he knew me already."

I rub my temple with my fingertips. "Is it worth taking the chance? What if they use you as leverage against me?"

Ryder cradles my hands in his. "I am not going to spend time apart from you because of them. I want to be with you."

"Even with all this craziness?" My brow creases.

Ryder answers me with a kiss. Part of me wants our lips to linger, but I pull away. Michelle's death is too fresh and I need to move forward with our plans to protect Tammy.

I pull my hands from Ryder's and walk towards the driver's side. "Let's do a drive-by now. I think I'll be calmer if we go past Tammy's and I can feel Othilia there. But only once now. Hopefully, the police aren't there yet. I'm not sure it'll be a good idea to be seen there too often. We're hardly inconspicuous in this van."

If Othilia is at Tammy's then she's not tailing my friends and that's a good thing. My logic could be flawed. She could use one of her buddies—like whoever was driving the sedan. Buddies or a henchman? Does she have henchmen? They could be following Tammy and reporting back. But I sense that Othilia wouldn't want to leave this to anyone else because I wouldn't want to either.

"Okay." Ryder opens the driver's side door. "If I drive you can watch for Othilia."

I shoot my arm across his chest to stop him from getting in. "I'd rather you lay low, remember?"

He sighs, knowing better than to argue with me. "If

that is how you want it."

The oversized sunglasses and hat from Mackay are long gone. I have a second pair of sunnies and tuck my hair into a beanie. Neither of us utters a word as we make the drive to Tammy's. When we pull onto her street, Ryder slides down in his seat as far as he can go.

As we reach my sister's house, the tingling takes over my body. I resist the urge to say "she's here" in a creepy singsong voice. No need to alert Othilia that someone else is in the car with me. I pull into the driveway.

Ryder puts his hands up as if to ask, "What are you doing," but I indicate with field signals for him to stop, forgetting he doesn't know the military code. Instead I do the universal gesture for halt and then leave the car. I walk to the front door, drinking in everything about her home. Potted plants filled with herbs and chili plants line the concrete patio. A small pile of shoes are stacked beside a welcome mat.

I put on the act of a concerned sibling and rap my knuckles against the front door, glancing around as though I'm expecting trouble. There's some truth to that. I wait a few moments and knock again. It doesn't matter that I know there will be no answer. It's the show that's important.

Shifting to my left, I cup my hands around my eyes so that I can peer through the window. Seeing inside makes my heart ache for Mum and Dad. Photos of Tammy and her family line the walls. She's obviously adopted. Her mother has long brown hair that frames pale freckly skin. Her father has Asian features.

As much as I want to stay and soak up Tammy's life, I know it's safer to keep moving on. I return to the car, doing my best to appear dejected. After reversing out of the driveway, I concentrate on the road. I don't want to risk making eye contact with Othilia, wherever she's hiding.

The tingling is gone by the end of the street. I sigh with relief. She isn't following us. I tense again for a moment as a police car goes past me. The officer doesn't even glance our way. Ryder knows to wait and only returns to an upright position once we're a few blocks away.

"What was the go with that?" Ryder asks. It's one of the few times I've heard him annoyed at me.

"Driving past wasn't enough. I needed to make it convincing, to show Othilia that I still think Tammy is in Townsville." It would have been better to warn Ryder, but I only thought of the idea when we were there. It would have seemed suspicious if I had started talking to myself.

"So she was there?"

I nod. "I felt her the whole time. She didn't follow us."

Ryder watches the scenery from the window as I drive us back to the caravan park. Now there's nothing for us to do but wait to repeat the charade until Tammy hits the news.

CHAPTER 22

RYDER

THE MEDIA CATCHES ONTO the story of Tammy's disappearance quicker than we anticipate. The day after we fake her disappearance, the appeal for witnesses makes the media. We stay away from Tammy's, like Mishca planned, to avoid winding up on the police's radar. Othilia would have heard about the kidnapping, ensuring Tammy's parents are safe.

This appears to give Mishca little comfort. She bites the corner of her thumb and taps her foot as we watch Tammy's parents make a heartfelt plea via satellite from Sweden, begging for their daughter's safe return. She turns away from the television screen in the airport lounge when the morning talk show host asks a question that brings Tammy's mother a fresh round of tears.

I put down my coffee and place my hand on hers. "We did the right thing." I pause seeing her uneaten toast. "You should eat something."

Mishca has hardly eaten over the past few days.

When she takes her medication she eats, but it is only a few bites. Her mental state is fragile at best, and not having enough energy could lower her ability to function even more. This frustrates me as much as when she goes into soldier mode. Either way I cannot seem to reach her.

"Don't you think it's odd that Michelle hasn't been on the news?" Mishca asks, absentmindedly scraping butter across her toast.

"Maybe it took longer for the people to be notified — you know the whole missing for twenty-four hours thing. Whereas with Tammy they knew there was something wrong." I fight to keep my face and voice calm. But the expression on Mishca's face shows I have failed.

"Two girls, who are almost exactly alike in appearance, missing within forty-eight hours, how could they explain that? And what if people who know Andrea and me see the images of these 'missing' girls?"

There was no frantic phone call from Mishca's deceased sister like we did with Tammy, but her disappearance will have to be reported soon. The authorities might not know she is dead yet. And if they find her body, it will be minus the chip.

Everyone is meant to have a double, but seeing four people who look virtually identical is over the top. I doubt her creator would want this attention either. But what other outcome would there be if Wirth follows through with the terminations?

Mishca inhales sharply. She picks up the little packet of jam that came with her breakfast, but her arm pauses in mid-air as she stares at the television screen. A news segment plays. A murder has happened on Tammy's street, an elderly couple. Police speculate if it is related to her disappearance. The deceased couple's townhouse is a prime stakeout spot.

Mishca's face pales like she needs to throw up. "How could I share DNA with someone so cold and cruel?" Her whole body goes rigid. Her hand clenches tight and suddenly something red and sticky covers my face.

"Mishca!"

She stares at the now empty jam packet in her hand.

"Sorry," she whispers. "I'm going to clean up."

I ache to reassure her that everything will be okay, but she stands up and walks away from me, leaving me literally red-faced and alone.

CHAPTER 23

MISHCA

I KNOW RYDER IS TALKING to me, but I don't listen. My goal is the solitude of the bathroom. Anxiety creeps up my neck and heats my face. I can't beat her. I can't win. She's too ruthless. Tammy will die and I'll lose another sister.

My hand grips the basin. I stare at my borrowed face. This is something I will never to be able to escape. From the moment I was made, I was a part of this. I clean up and check my watch. It's getting close to boarding time.

Pull yourself together, Mishca. I turn on the taps and wash the stickiness away. Then I feel it—her—and I've got nowhere to run.

"Hello, Mishca." Othilia's tone is anything but pleasant.

Before I can move an inch, she pins me against the hard tile wall. I struggle, but she's too strong. I attempt to reach deep inside and find some energy reserves, but I'm running on empty.

"I don't know how you got to her before me, but I know it was you. Where is she?" She sneers.

"I don't know." I'm telling the truth. Othilia should be a human lie detector too and will know it. With any luck, she can't tell it's a technicality. We all agreed no communication unless it was an emergency, apart from a cryptic text message from whoever arrives in Brisbane first. *Smelly Belly needs a bath* means a safe arrival home.

"Why do you care for her? She's defective, weak, and useless." Othilia relaxes her grip so that her nails are no longer digging into me, like she bought my semi-truth. I struggle to keep relief off my face.

"She's my sister." I pause, searching for a way to get through to her. "We share the same mother, the same blood."

"I don't have a mother, just a cell donor. And those pitiful creatures you call sisters are simply defectives needing to be put down." She grins at me like a serial killer in a horror movie. I never want to smile like that.

"You're human too." I reason with her. "Just because you weren't born in the conventional sense doesn't mean you aren't human. You're just a despicable human." Probably shouldn't have said that. I harden my jaw, but my legs are trembling.

"I'm *more* than human. I'm the first of a new race. So are you if you choose to embrace it." Othilia laughs. "You really don't have a choice. He'll come for you and you'll do what he wants because that's what you were made for. Learn to enjoy death because you're going to be its messenger."

"Never!" I recoil from her. "I will never be like you. You make me sick."

Othilia's face twists with rage. After a moment, her anger turns to amusement.

"Poor Ryder left all alone, unprotected in the airport lounge. Maybe I should get my boys to collect him for me. I'm in need of another pet. My current one is getting a bit worn out."

"Leave him al—" My protest is cut short by a backhand to my cheek. The force of the blow slams my head against the tiles. Black haze blurs my vision. I slip down the wall to the ground.

"Toodles," Othilia says in a horrible singsong. Her retreating footsteps are the only sound my ears can focus on.

My cheek burns. I want to race to Ryder, but I can barely move. I can't hear her anymore. *Get up. Move.* I will my body forward, to go to Ryder. My muscles don't cooperate. I squeeze my eyes shut and block every sensation I can.

I flinch as a hand touches my shoulder.

"Tammy? Are you Tammy Kanter?" A middle-aged blond woman stares at me with concerned eyes.

I manage a feeble shake of the head. She thinks I'm the "missing girl." Thinking fast, I feign an American accent. The words hurt my throat, but I force them free anyway. "No." I can't keep the tainted warble from my voice. "I'm Mishca. Mishca Richardson."

The blond woman hovers around, keeping an eye on me. I'm not sure if she's convinced I'm Tammy or if she's concerned about me regardless. My body finally decides it can move. I push up, go to the basin, and splash some water on my face. In the mirror I see the stinging red mark on my right cheek from Othilia's hand.

A crackly voice calls over the public announcement system. "Final call for passengers Ryder Madson and Mishca Richardson. Your plane is awaiting immediate departure. Please make your way to gate four."

I race from the restroom, searching for Ryder, but he's not at our table. My hands screw up into balls of panic.

"Mishca. Hey. We have got to go." Ryder is to my left, leaning on the wall outside the restrooms, our bags in hand, completely at ease with my pink handbag.

"Ryder!"

Before I can hug him, he clutches my arm and drags me towards gate four, oblivious to my distress.

Ryder hands over our boarding passes to the gate attendant and passes me my handbag. She gives us a knowing, sympathetic smile. She must see people rushing for a plane regularly. The other passengers are not so friendly. Plenty of them glare at us as we enter the plane. I'm relieved our seats are not far along.

"Here, you take the window." Ryder sidesteps and lets me through first.

I slide across, placing my handbag under the seat. When I clip my seatbelt on, I hear Ryder take a sharp breath.

"What happened to your face?" He's on my right and can see the mark left by my sister.

"Othilia." I do not meet his gaze.

"Here? When? What happened?" he asks frantically.

"She cornered me in the toilet." I turn to face him. "She thinks I know where Tammy is." My voice stays low. "She also threatened you." I stare at the tarmac, wishing I were anywhere but here.

"Oh, Mishca." Code for, *Oh, shit, I screwed up.* "You should have said something."

"There wasn't time." I squeeze my eyes shut and take a deep breath before looking back at Ryder. "It's okay. How were you to know? I didn't sense her at all until she came at me. It's like she snuck up on me."

Airplane sitting does little to help a couple when they want to kiss and make up. Not that it was a major fight or anything, but all I want right now is to snuggle up next to my boyfriend with no one else around and no seatbelts and armrests to get in our way.

"That is going to make things hard when we get back." He grabs a pen and paper from the seat pocket in front of him and then writes, *Tony is going to have to keep a really low profile.*

Othilia knows we're heading home and she'll be watching us like hawks. I'm hoping she'll focus more on me than my boyfriend.

I manage a nod. He screws up the paper, shoving it into the sick bag. My mind races through different scenarios.

"We're going to have to act as though we're carrying on as normal," I whisper back. "She *has* been watching us. If we suddenly become recluses, she'll know something's up."

The safety message interrupts before he can respond. He closes his mouth and his eyes fix forward on the flight attendant. Ryder's jaw stays set tight through the pre-take-off talk and the captain's announcements as we ascend into the clouds.

"She cannot stay with me," he says once we're settled in the flight path.

"Why? Don't you want her there?" I can't hide my hurt.

"She will be in danger."

I cock my head. "What do you mean?"

"Othilia knows about me and will be watching us both. What will happen if she knows you are not at my place and she gets that tingling feeling anyway?"

My whole body deflates like a slowly leaking balloon. Where else can I cache Tammy without exposing her? She can't stay at Nerissa's or Dylan's. The only other people who know are Connor and Fin. I don't know if Connor's parents would let him bring in some random stranger and the situation with Fin is far too sticky to contemplate. "We're screwed."

"We will think of something," Ryder says as the food trolley rattles our way.

"Something to eat or drink?" the flight attendant asks.

"No, thanks." I let Ryder answer for the both of us.

My mind drifts to Andrea over in Europe with no idea of the drama unfolding here. We have to warn her...somehow. She knew Michelle was living in Mackay. Maybe they made contact. No, Michelle had no idea about any doubles when Othilia struck. Then, it hits me. I think I'll be able to contact Andrea, but it'll have to wait until I get home.

I press the button to tilt my chair back and close my eyes, wondering how we can escape this mess.

CHAPTER 24

RYDER

BEING APART FROM HER now is killing me. I want to be with her, protect her, despite knowing she can do a better job of that than I can. I got lucky in Airlie Beach when I managed to zap Othilia. I do not even know if I can do it again.

Jelly Roll jumps around my feet, letting his slobber drip onto me as I slide the key into the lock. I reach down and scoop him into my arms. His tongue lashes my face, leaving sticky saliva trails. Obviously, Connor has been feeding him while I have been away as he weighs down my arms. I let him lick me a couple more times before placing him on the ground and opening the door.

Immediately, I sense another presence in the room. My internal energy stays at bay, which takes me even more by surprise.

"You wanted to talk." Sophitia's voice slides over me like silk.

I should have jumped, should have blasted her with

a bolt on instinct, sent her flying across the room because I did not know it was my cousin when I came in. Or maybe my subconscious knew she was not the threat I had feared.

She sits on the beanbag. Her lace purple dress puffs around her.

"Tell me about my mother." I opt for authoritative rather than demanding.

"The visit with Rosie did not go well I take it?" Sophitia curls her hand towards her, inspecting her nails and then glances up at me as though she wishes to gauge my reaction.

"She is not my mother."

She does not even flinch. "You had Mishca there. Did Rosie lie about giving you up for adoption?"

"Well, no, but she is not the woman I remember. Tell me what is going on."

Sophitia puts her hands down to push herself up. "I am not in a position to tell you. And you should leave this alone. Yes, I am your cousin. And your mother asked me to watch over you. That is all I can tell you."

I squeeze my eyelids shut for a moment and inhale. *Why will she not talk to me?* A ball of frustration bounces around in my stomach. I contemplate asking her if she knows why I glow blue, but decide it is best not to expose my secret, just in case. "Talk to me, please. I have a right to know the truth about my real parents."

She lowers her head. "You would think so. But it is not for me to say. I will be there for you any other way I can. I cannot help you on the topic of your mother."

"Pfft. Do you know how lame that sounds? You

have the opportunity to fill a hole in my life. To help me find the rest of my family. And you are straight up refusing. I cannot believe you."

Sophitia turns from me. "You need to listen to more words, more carefully." Then, she saunters off through the door.

As though it was waiting for Sophitia to leave, my energy ignites, sparking all over my skin. Not wanting to destroy everything in my living room, I breathe and push everything down. I sit cross-legged, ready to meditate. I let calmness ripple over me, smothering the anger before it can get the better of me.

I almost lost it when we were at the cloning facility. The feeling was not as strong then as it has been lately, fuelling my fear that I am like Mishca and have been activated.

Shoving any negativity away, I focus on the positives. I have Mishca back, and nothing will come between us again.

"Ryder."

My eyes pop open. Finlay stands before me, grinning hesitantly.

"Hey." His voice is mixed with apprehension and hope. None of the venom he showed in our last encounter is evident at all.

The only word I can find is an echo of his. "Hey."

He glances away abashed and rubs the back of his neck with his hand.

I clear my throat. "What have you been up to?"

He puts his hand out palms up. "You know, being an ass…as usual."

"Ah-ha." I will always choose Mishca, but if Finlay is back and ready to make nice, I will not turn him away. Does not mean I will make it easy for him.

"I was out of line with Mishca. It brought so much stuff to the surface for me about my dad and I acted like a complete cretin."

I simply cock an eyebrow, keeping my face straight even though I am laughing inside.

"Come on, man. What do I have to do?"

Then, it comes to me. A way to use this to my advantage, and test if he is serious about making amends. "Help Mishca."

Finlay's Adam's apple bobs when he gulps, but he nods. "How?"

I fill him in on the trip, every detail I can without revealing my light show. I know I can trust him, but we are dealing with enough. And I have totally dug a hole. How can I tell him now when I have known for years that I spark energy?

Fin nods throughout the whole thing as though he is on autopilot.

"So Tammy is coming with Mishca's evil twin on the lookout. We need to keep her safe. Chances are she will not be safe here. Can she hide at your place?"

"You know it." He extends a fist. I bump it. And as simple as that, all is good between us.

CHAPTER 25

MISHCA

"MISHCA, LUNCH IN FIVE minutes," Mum calls to me as I float on my back in our pool. I've been home for two days, doing what I can to keep my mind off the fact that there's been no text message from Nerissa yet. They should have made it by now. I've hardly seen anything of Ryder as I insist he stay on sentinel duty.

I breaststroke to the side of the pool and climb onto the tiles. I dry off, wrap a towel around my chest, and pick up my phone. There's still no message. Flipping through the apps, I go onto the fake Facebook page I created for Michelle Cooper. There's no reply from Andrea yet either. I figured that she would be more receptive to a friend request from the girl she's been stalking in Mackay. There was too much of a risk of freaking her with one from another lookalike from Brisbane.

Lunch smells delicious. Roast duck, my favorite. Plopping onto a chair, I pile up my plate. I've barely eaten over the last week and it's caught up with me.

Probably why I couldn't take Othilia on. I refuse to give any thought to the notion that I can't beat her in a fair fight.

Smelly Belly thinks the food smells pretty good too. She rubs around my legs purring, hoping I'll sneak her a bit of duck. Of course, I do.

"Mishca, really. Could you not sit at the table all wet?" Mum complains, pointing to the damp patch I've made on the seat covers. Honestly, who thought suede was a good idea for dining chairs?

"Fine." I push my chair and stomp upstairs to put on a fresh set of clothes.

Dad passes me as I reach my bedroom. "Is Ryder coming for lunch today?"

Dad has taken more of a liking to Ryder. I think it's because he saw how low I got after I discovered my "birth parents" and knows that it was Ryder who pulled me from my funky pity party.

"No, he's working today." I'm not referring to the Fitness Factory. Ryder's job is to stay at home and wait to see if Tammy and the others turn up.

Suitably attired in dry shorts and a T-shirt, I return to the table, cell phone in hand. It's been like an extension of my arm since I've gotten home. I sit in a different seat so I don't get my shorts wet.

My spirits lift watching my mum and dad with their playful banter. It was only once I got back that I realized how much I missed them. Nothing changes; they're my parents, no matter how I came into being. They raised me, loved me, and gave me a home.

"So the uni applications for next year close soon."

Dad casts a sly grin. "Are you excited to get back into it?"

Uni! It hasn't crossed my mind in ages. Poor Tammy. She'll probably get an automatic incomplete on her classes, unless some bright spark in administration takes pity on her. Then again, I don't even know if she's at uni, or if she is, when she'll be able to go back. In all the madness I didn't even ask. I put in my application—at universities where Professor Colin Reed does not teach—but I am doubtful I'll go. Too much is unknown. That familiar, but faded pang hits my heart at the thought of Colin.

"Yeah, sure. It'll be a blast," I mumble through a mouthful of salad. Not thrilled at the notion of being a university freshman again, constantly glancing over my shoulder, waiting for this Wirth guy to decide it's time for me to fight. *Woo. Frickin. Hoo.*

"Have you thought about what you might like to study next year?" Mum asks.

"I'm still thinking public relations or journalism." Being a human lie detector could come in handy in the media field.

Dad screws up his nose. He's had some run-ins with journalists at post-match press conferences. "Are you sure? Have you considered law or accounting?"

I put my finger in my mouth and pretend to gag. "You want me to die of boredom?"

Before my parents can answer my phone beeps with a text message.

Smelly Belly needs a bath!

"Oh, ah, um, I gotta go. Ryder's got the afternoon

off work. Got to make the most of this time before we're both back at school." I shove some more roast duck in my mouth and snatch my keys off the counter.

"Don't make too much of it," Dad calls as I sprint toward the garage.

I'm on cloud nine. *She's here! She's here!* And she's safe.

I pause as I reverse from the driveway. I've felt Othilia a couple of times, but she has been careful to keep her distance. Today, I don't feel her at all. I hope that means she's not around. Regardless, I scan my surroundings for any sign.

During the drive to Ryder's house, I check for vehicles following me every few seconds. I don't see any, but that doesn't stop me being on edge. The moment I hit the driveway, the tingles wash over me. Tammy must feel them too as she's hovering near the back door. She pounces on me with a hug the instant I come inside.

"What took you so long to get here?" I hug her tight back. "I was so worried."

Tammy grimaces. "The van broke down in Emerald. We had to wait for the hire company to send a replacement."

Her hair has sprung up to her ears with kinks kicking in. It'll be like mine again soon thanks to the makeshift haircut Nerissa gave her in Townsville. She's wearing some of Ryder's clothes that are way too big for her. Her wig and hairnet rest on the table.

"I've been trying to contact Andrea through Facebook, but she hasn't responded yet." I'm little-miss-one-track-mind.

"Don't you think she'll be freaked getting a message from a doppelganger?" she asks, her voice filled with concern.

"Maybe from a Mishca Richardson twin, but one from Michelle Cooper should be okay." I shrug. "At least that's my theory. She knew about Michelle and had been tracking her. But I don't think she knows much else."

"Has she been online since you sent the message?" She reaches for non-existent long hair and rubs her hand against her bare neck instead with a frown.

"I don't know."

Strong arms grab me from behind, lifting me off my feet and swirling me around. Ryder lets me slide from his arms, greeting me with his lips on mine once my feet touch the ground. Even a few days without seeing each other feels like too long.

A discreet cough from Tammy breaks us apart. I give her an embarrassed smile.

"Oh, don't mind me. I've got nothing better to do than watch you two smooch." She tries to keep a straight face, but a chuckle tugs at the corner of her mouth.

I can't help but smirk. The two of us break into giggles, leaving a bewildered Ryder shaking his head. It's so hard to keep my hands off him. We've purposely spent little time together the last two days, not wanting to risk drawing Othilia over here. Even though he gave Tammy a key, I was still freaked that we beat our friends home and wanted him to be there when they arrived.

"Come on." Tammy tugs at my arm. "We're putting on a movie."

Ryder's pocket vibrates. He snags his phone and peeks at the screen. "You guys start without me. I need to take this."

I let Tammy lead me into the lounge room. It's all set up for a veg session with lollies, chocolate, popcorn, and drinks.

Jelly Roll must have missed me too. He waddles over with a lopsided grin and plops himself at my feet, and then flops onto his back. I oblige, rubbing his belly. His tongue hangs loose and his leg twitch. Tammy picks up the remote and puts on the TV. It's still set to the news. Ryder's been watching for anything on Michelle.

Tammy and I both reach for the block of hazelnut chocolate. She gets to it first and breaks some off for me.

"It's my favorite." I pop it in my mouth.

"Me too," Tammy manages to utter through her mouthful of chocolate.

Jelly Roll gives some appreciative grunts.

Tammy licks her fingers so they're chocolate free and then picks up two DVDs.

"Which one?" she asks, holding up a romantic comedy in her left hand and a horror in her right.

"That one." I point to her left. We've been in enough frightening situations.

The side of Tammy's mouth quirks. "All right then, cats or dogs?"

"Cats." I glance at Ryder's pudgy dog. "No offence, Jelly Roll."

He lifts his head, snorts as though to dismiss my comment, and plops back down.

"Okay." Tammy snags another piece of chocolate. "Favorite subject at school?"

"Society and Culture."

"Mine too. I also love cats." Tammy grins.

Ryder comes into the room and sits on the lounge. He must have overheard some of the conversation and understood because he doesn't interrupt us. He watches us instead with amusement.

"Worst subject at school?" I ask.

"Ugh, math." Tammy screws up her nose like I do when confronted with a complex equation, and then asks, "Favorite season?"

"Spring." I grin. "I love the flowers, all the baby animals, and how everything smells so good."

Tammy nods at my words.

"What were you studying at uni?"

"Journalism. I had considered drama, but my parents were worried it wouldn't give me job security."

I nod at the similarities, but am disappointed at how much this is screwing up her life.

"Favorite sport," she asks, obviously enjoying the game.

"Rugby league." Growing up with Dad playing it and then coaching it, and not being able to participate in sports myself, gave me little other choice.

"Really?" Tammy screws up her nose as if I had told her I like licking toads. "Mine's hockey. I made the

Townsville rep team in high school."

"No way. Are you serious?" I never aspired to anything like that with my health. Having her heart transplant earlier than me must have opened up a lot more doors.

"Yep. I love it. I don't mind watching rugby league though."

"Well, I guess some things are environmental, not genetic." I shrug, not wanting to make a big deal of it.

Before I can think of another question, there's a knock at the door and I freeze. My veins feel like they're filled with ice. Tammy and I stare at each other in horror.

"Hide!" I hiss.

CHAPTER 26

RYDER

TAMMY CROUCHES AND scuttles across the floor, past the TV and into the bedroom. Mishca stays frozen like a statue until her sister is nowhere in sight before joining me near the door. She wipes at her face with her hands and then uses her shorts to dry them.

"Be cool, Mishca." I had forgotten to warn her that Fin would be coming over.

I turn the handle and open the door to reveal a stern-faced Finlay on the other side. Mishca pulls me back, getting up on tiptoes and cupping her hand around my ear.

"You have to get rid of him," she whispers. "If he loses it and makes a scene, Tammy could be in real danger. What if Othilia's watching us?"

"It's okay, Mishca," Fin says, totally ignoring that she doesn't want him here. "I'm here to help."

Mishca's body tenses at his words.

Have I done the right thing?

Finlay closes the door and then goes over and taps

at my room. "It's okay, Tammy. I'm not here to hurt you."

"What's going on?" Mishca asks.

"Fin came over when I got home. He apologized for being an arse." I raise an eyebrow; he returns it with a sheepish smile. "I told him if he wanted to make it up to you he could help us hide Tammy."

Mishca folds her arms and quirks an eyebrow. "What's your mum going to think?"

Fin shrugs. "Mum's happy to have me home. She never complains when I bring a girl around. She's never seen you, so she won't know what's up."

Tammy opens the bedroom door and peers out. Fin gasps at the sight of her.

"Y-you look just like her," he stammers.

A real Sherlock Holmes here.

"That's what happens when you clone someone." Tammy raises an unimpressed eyebrow that mimics Mishca's previous facial expression to the letter. Without warning, she swears and points at the TV.

Tammy turns up the volume as the rest of us gape. The voice of a serious-faced female presenter is the only sound in the room.

"Mackay police have identified the body as that of seventeen-year-old Michelle Cooper." An image flashes on the screen and my stomach lurches. "No suspects have been identified and any witnesses are asked to come forward."

It's not my girlfriend's face staring back at me from the TV screen.

"It's not her. Why is it not her?" Mishca whispers.

"What's going on?" Fin asks.

"Michelle Cooper is one of us. She's the one Othilia killed in Mackay." Mishca says it like she is talking to a pre-schooler.

"But that chick wasn't anything like you guys. I mean, you know, she was still similar, but there's no way she was a clone."

"They're covering their tracks." Mishca chews on her thumbnail.

"That makes some sense." Tammy mimics Mishca unknowingly. When she catches sight of her sister's stance she drops her hand from her mouth. "Heck of a lot of work though."

"Let's worry about those details later." Fin waves a hand at the TV like he is dismissing the news. "I think the important thing is you guys are all back in town now and we need to get Tammy over to my place ASAP."

"So how are we going to get her there safely?" Mishca folds her arms over her chest.

Othilia seems to have learned the right distance to trail us to stay off the clone radar, complicating things. The airport incident is proof of that. But we can do this.

"I am going to drive us to Fin's. Tammy will need to stay under a blanket in the back until we get inside the garage," I say, sure this will work.

"But the garage is separate to the house and we could be spotted crossing the yard." Mishca's eyebrows furrow.

"Easy. I drive the car up to the porch," I say with triumph that falters at Mishca's stern face.

Fin goes with Tammy to the linen cupboard to get a blanket.

"You could have warned me." Mishca makes no effort to hide the annoyance in her voice.

"How? We agreed no texts or calls mentioning Tammy." My brows pinch together.

She sighs. "I'm sorry. I'm so on edge."

"I know, babe." I pull her to me and kiss the top of her head.

Fin and Tammy return with a large blanket. It is going to be hot under that thing.

Mishca turns to Fin. "What made you change your mind?"

"I realized you're like my family too. Connor and I went through the files. They gave my dad the genetic enhancements while he was in the army, before I was born. He was part of some super soldier program. The doctors who were working on him left the military to work for Wirth and they gave you and your sisters that same treatment. What flows in my veins, flows in your veins." He shrugs. "Besides, I was a jerk."

Tammy laughs as she puts her wig on. "Sure sounds like it."

I smirk as I walk towards my car. Finlay deserves everything he gets. My pace is even, level, giving no indication there is anything wrong. I make sure I do everything like I normally would.

Mischca, Finlay, and Tammy are silhouettes in the doorframe as I ease the car as close as I can to the house.

"Wait." Mishca strides out before the others. She

squints, scans the yard, and then steps outside, signalling for the others to stay put. She heads over to me and I wind the window down.

"I'm going to do a quick perimeter sweep," she says softly, sounding too calm. But I can see the nervousness in her face. "Othilia was set up in a house across from Tammy's in Townsville. She could've done that here too. If I walk around your fence line I should be able to feel if she's in one of your neighbor's houses."

I give a stern nod, not wanting any super hearing to pick up a conversation. She dashes around the edge of the property and then disappears from sight at a speed that has to be seen to be believed. Tension releases from my shoulders and I make my way to the others.

"Not a single hair on edge." Mishca should be smiling, but she is back in soldier mode. 'She's not in the immediate vicinity."

My best friend and girlfriend go into signal mode. Fin seems to be following Mishca's instructions. He opens the car's back door. Once he has indicated it is all clear, Mishca signals to the blanket-covered Tammy.

Tammy ducks into the car, diving in and squeezing down between the front and back seats. Mishca jumps in behind her, tucking the blanket in around her sister.

"Oi, front seat, missy." Fin gestures with his head for Mishca to move. "It'd be weird if you were in the back."

Mishca straddles the seats, and slides across onto the passenger side. Thank goodness she is wearing shorts today. No need to give Finlay a show like he got on our first date.

Fin closes the back door and opens the passenger door. "Move across."

"What? Why?" Mishca protests, probably remembering how awkward the last drive was like this.

"If these people have been following you, then they could have seen us on the drive home that night," I say as softly as possible. "Fin's right. We need to be consistent."

"Fine." She sighs, scooching across and throwing her leg over the gear stick.

Fin gives an appreciative grin. Mishca glares at him like she thinks maybe things were better when he was not talking to her. I frown, but this is not the time to make a scene.

"I've also spoken to Nerissa today," Fin says as we pull onto the road. "It's got to seem like you guys are back to normal life. She got passes to her Uncle's nightclub tonight. I'll stay in and look after Tammy. You guys go out and throw them off her scent."

"Normally, I would love the chance to go to the Bowl," Mishca says. "But—"

"You know that is the best thing to do." My hand moves between her legs to change gears.

She throws up her hands in surrender. "Okay. We go to the Bowl tonight."

Fin's lives only ten minutes away in a nice suburb filled with brick homes. Most of the yards have manicured gardens, a typical middle-class area. As I steer into the driveway, Fin activates the automatic garage door with his key ring. It groans and shudders open. I maneuver the car inside. We wait until the door has closed again.

"That was disgusting." Tammy pops her sweating head from under the blanket.

Fin grabs a towel from an airing rack at the back of the garage. "Here." He passes it to her.

"We better not stay long." I glance at the door that connects the garage to the house. "Last thing we need is for your mum to see Tammy and Mishca together."

Mishca and her sister hug before Tammy and Fin go through the connecting door to the house. Fin leaves it open a crack, enough to watch as he reopens the garage for us. When we are on the road, the door rattles shut.

I stare at Mishca. She chews on her lip. This is the second time she has had to leave Tammy and put on a show. Will her life ever get back to normal?

CHAPTER 27

MISHCA

BREATHE. PRETEND LIKE nothing's wrong. Get back to a normal life. I repeat the mantra over and over again as we walk into the Bowl. The bass is throbbing, filling the air, and leading the people on the dance floor to sway in time with its beat. I spot Connor with a group of friends and give him an awkward wave as Ryder, Nerissa, Dylan, and I weave through of the mass of dancers to our private booth. Happiness is plastered on my face, pulling my cheeks so tight it hurts. The strobe lights flicker off the sequins on my dress as we all sit. I'm dazzling on the outside, but my fear for Tammy's safety has hollowed me. Nerissa and Dylan have already caught the beat bug, bouncing around in their seats.

"Do you want to come and dance?" Nerissa yells over the music.

"Nah, I'm thirsty." I add the appropriate hand movements to ensure my message gets across.

"Do you want me to get them?" Ryder asks.

"That'd be great."

Ryder bends so he can whisper in my ear. "By the way, you look so hot."

A blush rises and I give my first genuine smile of the night. I do love my outfit tonight. It's a strapless electric blue sequined party dress that sits mid-thigh. It shows off my legs nicely, and I no longer care if people see my scar. My cross necklace and the earrings from Ryder are my only jewellery.

As Ryder makes his way over to the bar, Nerissa leans in. "So how is she?"

This is the first time we've been able to catch up since we've gotten back from Townsville.

"Good. I think Fin will take care of her," I say.

I don't think we have to be worried we'll be overheard. We can barely hear each other. I glance at the bar. Ryder has made his way through the front of the line and puts his order in with a white-haired bartender.

"Finlay?" Nerissa is almost as taken aback as I was. "How did that happen?"

"Who's Finlay?" Dylan pipes in.

"Ryder's best friend." I get in first. "He came over to Ryder's to set things right. When he found out about Tammy, he offered to help. His mum's place shouldn't be on Othilia's radar."

Ryder returns with a tray full of drinks. I help him unload the glasses around the table, putting the Cinderella mocktail in front of me. The others have piña coladas.

"That was quick." Dylan picks the little umbrella

from his drink. He discards it onto the table as though it offends him.

"Yeah. You get good service when they see you coming over from the VIP booth." Ryder raises his glass. "Cheers."

"Cheers," we chorus, clinking our glasses together.

The cool liquid hits my throat and a calm settles over me. My worries evaporate. The sugar buzz from the mocktail gives me the motivation to get up and boogie. When I've emptied the contents of my glass, I take hold of Ryder's arm and yank him onto the dance floor.

A pair of breasts that go with green hair and a smirk block my path.

"Hey, sugarplum." Sophitia plants one on me. "You taste good. What have you been drinking, virgin Sex on the Beach?"

My jaw drops. I struggle to find a witty response.

"Leave her alone," Ryder says.

Sophitia turns to Ryder and simpers. "Oh, you are no fun. Did no one teach you the importance of sharing?"

She blows us both kisses before slinking off into the crowd.

"Sorry. Sophitia can be an ass sometimes." Ryder's face drops as though he's worried my dancing buzz has faded. But it hasn't.

"It's fine." I can't wipe the grin off my face. She hasn't gotten to me. I want to let loose.

Ryder snakes his arms around my waist and steers me into the crowd of dancers.

"Forget about her." His eyes gleam in the strobe lights. "Forget about everything. Just dance."

"Less talking, more grooving." I give Ryder a sassy push.

I let go, feeling the music running through my body. Ryder reaches for me again, and this time, I let him keep a hold of me. I enjoy the sensation of our hips pressing against each other in time to the beat.

After an hour, my body hasn't tired, but I'm yearning big time for something else. I pull Ryder to the edge of the dancers and then into the shadows. There's a heat inside me that I have to set free. My hands grasp his shirt, harder than I mean to as there's a bit of a ripping sound, and bring his body against mine. Our foreheads touch. I stare into his eyes, willing him to know what I want. Our breathing is sharp.

Ryder gives me what I want, and moves his lips onto mine. He starts off soft, but I kiss him back hungrily. I feel the warmth of him too. The tiny sparks jump from his fingertips and leap onto my skin, creating a rippling pleasure that creeps over all my body.

Ryder leans back and stares at me, his eyes flashing purple again. I motion to a nearby empty table. Sitting on it, I beckon him with my finger to join me, ignoring the gawks from the people at the table beside us. I lick my lips, wondering why I've been so shy with Ryder before now. I love his touch, the excitement, being out of control. Once he's close enough, I reach up to lock my fingers around his neck. As our mouths connect again, my body arches towards him.

I take his hand from my hip and move it to my thigh. It would be better if we were alone at Ryder's place. Part of me wants to rush off there right now, but the music keeps dancing inside my head. It feels so good, I don't want to leave. Our kisses deepen, and I move his hand further up so it's under my dress.

This time Ryder retreats from our embrace.

"Not here. Not like this."

I pout. It does little to sway him. He stares at me like I've said I want to do harm to kittens. He's spoiling the party. I move in again, but he pulls away.

"Come on. We should see how the others are doing." Ryder skirts around the dance floor this time.

The club spins in front of me and nausea grips my body like a clamp wound too tight. I clutch Ryder's arm to keep steady.

Back at the table Nerissa and Dylan are both mopping sweat from their brows, not long off the dance floor either.

"You guys are such party poopers." I moan and put on my best sad face. My gaze is drawn to a couple making out on the dance floor. I want that to be me.

"Excuse me." The white-haired server is standing by our table with a tray of aqua drinks. "These are compliments of the lady over there."

He points at Sophitia, who gives us a big smirk. Sophitia and her friends raise their glasses, full of the same aqua liquid, as if to say "cheers" and then promptly scull them. They all hoot and slam their glasses on the table, laughing.

"Can we get another round of what we had before

too, please?" I bat my eyelashes and pass him some cash.

"Sure thing." A wicked grin crosses his lips. His eyes flash purple in the lights. Heat rises in my face and I giggle.

Dylan rubs his hands together. "Oh, yeah!"

Nerissa sniffs the drink. Seemingly satisfied, she raises her glass. We all raise ours, tapping them together in celebration.

Dylan, Nerissa, and Ryder follow Sophitia's lead and throw back their heads, draining the contents. I take a tentative sip. My throat burns in protest.

"Not again," Nerissa splutters. "Bloody absinthe."

"Why do people want to drink this stuff?" Dylan says before going into a coughing fit.

"Here you go." The server has made it back superfast with our other drinks.

"Thanks." I give him a wink.

Ryder glances between the two of us with a frown. I flash him my best everything-is-okay face. I feel great. My super-soldier is nowhere in sight.

I take a tentative sip of my Cinderella. Definitely non-alcoholic. While I doubt I need to stick to the heart-transplant recovery instructions, some habits die hard. I drink my mocktail as quickly as possible, hoping to get rid of the acidic absinthe taste. My friends blur in front of my eyes and my stomach churns. The room turns stuffy and hot.

"I think I'm going to be sick. I've got to go to the loo," I say in a low voice.

Ryder cocks a brow. His lips move, but I don't hear

anything.

I stumble my way through the throng of people. My sense of direction is on the fritz. I retreat to a corner and take three deep breaths. When I open my eyes, the server with the white hair is bent over me, staring. His face has sharp, high cheekbones and almond-shaped eyes that mimic Ryder's.

"You do not look too good." His face looks pleasant, but his eyes twinkle with malice. "I should take you home."

I can't find the strength to resist when he takes my hand and easily pulls me to my feet. His strength is surprising for his lean frame. He leads me through the front door, not pausing when I stumble. Everything goes fuzzy. I can feel the night air and his hand on me.

"Here, get in," he orders.

"No." I drop from his grasp and deliver an elbow to his stomach. But it's given sloppily with my decline in senses.

I've been drugged.

"Baby, it is time for you to see Wirth." His voice isn't kind anymore.

I blink, refocusing. More hands are on my body, pushing me towards a car. I scream a split second before my head connects with the vehicle's roof. Grey splotches blur my vision and then everything goes black.

CHAPTER 28

RYDER

I WATCH MISHCA DISAPPEARING amongst the partying people and cannot shake the feeling that something is not right. But I know better this time than to follow my girlfriend into the ladies room.

Sophitia and her friends slide into the booth. I want so badly to talk to her about my mum, but now is not the right time. Instead, I sit and brood in my anxiousness. Fear grips my insides like an MMA fighter, twisting hard.

Glasses are raised with a clink, but I stay silent, my drink on the table.

I snatch my phone from my pocket and check the time. Mishca has been gone for fifteen minutes. Too long. The conversation around me becomes background noise, blending with the music. I stand and take a step, but turn to Nerissa.

"I think something is wrong. Mishca has not come back from the toilet. Come with me to check on her?"

Nerissa gulps and nods. She whispers to Dylan,

slides out of the booth, and follows me through the throng. We get to the other side and Nerissa pushes through the door with the silhouette of a busty girl badged on the outside. Moments later she comes back, eyes wide, head shaking. A ball of energy swells inside me, pulsing, pushing to escape. I breathe in, like inhaling air will extinguish it. It does not.

I run. Shoving people. Knocking over drinks. Leaving a stream of pissed off patrons in my wake. When a bouncer's hand clamps on my shoulder and propels me towards the exit, he simply serves to expedite my journey.

The cool night air wraps around me. I ignore it and search for any sign of Mishca. I pause and listen. To my right, I am sure of it, though I cannot explain why. I run further down the street, stopping on a dime in front of a man in a green tie who cocks his head at me.

"Have you seen a girl in a blue sequined dress?" My description is so vague I am not expecting a positive response.

"Yes, I have. A group of men were forcing her into a car parked in the alley across the street."

I shoot him a venomous glare. "Why did you let them take her?"

He shrugs. "Not my place."

I swallow down bile and sprint across the street. The energy inside expands. The blue glow pushes at my skin.

A scream echoes into the night as I spot the car. Its lights are on and the engine is running. My mind is too foggy with fear to comprehend that the car is moving forward until it connects with my body, sending me to the ground with a thump. My head bounces on the pavement and the impact dampens everything. All I can do is lay on the sidewalk as the fuzzy red lights grow smaller and Mishca gets further away.

"Ryder, are you okay?" Nerissa's blue eyes search my face.

I groan as my body protests my attempts to sit up.

"Dude, stay still. An ambulance is on the way." I think Dylan is talking to me.

Determination grips me and I shake off the pain, gingerly getting to my feet. "She is gone. They took her."

"Mishca!" Nerissa's voice is laced with fear. "Who took her? Dylan, call the police."

"Ryder, what is going on?" Sophitia places a gentle hand on my shoulder.

I stare at my cousin. "What did you do to her?" It is a big jump to accuse Sophitia of drugging my girlfriend, but Mishca's behavior matched.

"What do you mean?" Her eyes widen at my accusation.

"You paid for our drinks and there was a special one for Mishca." My tone remains harsh.

"Wait," Nerissa cuts in. "You think Mishca's drink was spiked?"

I ignore the question and keep glaring at Sophitia.

"That drink was not from me," Sophitia whispers. "The guy behind the bar added it to my tray. He said you had paid for it earlier. I did not even know she could drink alcohol because of her heart."

My head finds my hands and I slump back to the ground.

"I should have protected her." The energy has totally dissipated. I stare longingly down the street again, hoping to see her face. Instead my eyes see a church, lit up and open. A figure lingers in the doorway. Maybe they saw something. And if ever there was a time to pray, this is it.

"Ryder, where are you going?" Sophitia calls when I head down the street.

"To pray." I point to the church. The figure disappears inside. "Tell the police where I am when they get here."

The scenery around me fades to nothing. I have failed her. I should have kept her safe. If only I had reacted faster, realized sooner. The church is old and weathered, but upon stepping inside I can see it is well maintained. It reminds me a lot of the Anglican churches I went to with my parents as I grew up. I cannot remember when I stopped attending with them, probably about the time my father and I had the fall out about my future.

"Hello? Anyone here?" I wish I had Mishca's heightened senses right now. I pace around, checking every spot where someone could have slipped into shadows, but find no one. The area behind the pulpit is the only place I do not go. It feels wrong to violate that area.

I find a pew at the back of the church. Sitting down, I begin to pray furiously. I beg for forgiveness for not protecting Mishca and for her safety. When I raise my head towards the ceiling in a final plea to have her back with me, I see a priest walking towards me from the front of the church.

He sits beside me, warmth and kindness radiating off him. "Are you lost my son? Or have you lost?"

I shift uncomfortably. "I have lost someone...and I want her back. I was hoping he could help." I point skyward.

"People often seek refuge in the arms of our Lord in times of need. That is understandable, but we cannot expect him to intervene whenever we hit trouble." Something is off in his voice. "Sometimes we have to take responsibility for our actions, wills, and desires. We can turn to him when we are lost. When we lose someone—"

"I did not exactly lose someone." I snap like I have been wound too tight. "She was taken from me forcibly."

"Really now. And what would you give to get her back?" The priest glances at me. I shift uncomfortably in my seat.

"Just about anything."

"Deal." The priest presents me with his hand. My jaw slackens. *What is he talking about?* Instinctively, my hand reaches forward and grips his open palm. The deal is done.

"Zuriel," the priest calls to someone unseen. "Do you have Mishca's position?"

My head jerks to the right.

The grey man in the long trench coat that assisted us at EEF—and later assaulted us—steps from a side room, holding something in his hand.

"You!" I fly from my seat before the energy inside me even has time to react, throwing my fist at his jaw with all my might. A searing pain shoots through my hand and up my arm. It is like his jaw is made of stone; his head did not even move. A string of expletives fly from my lips while my hidden power surges beneath my skin.

"That was rather foolish, youngling." The grey man takes my hand and examines it. "It is fortuitous that you have not injured yourself more seriously."

Still clutching my hand, I turn to the priest. "I never told you her name was Mishca."

"I know." The priest smiles. "So Zuriel, do we know where they have taken her?"

My enthusiasm for violence against the man-mountain quells. For the first time I properly inspect the item in Zuriel's hand. It appears to be a GPS tracker.

"How did you…" My voice trails off.

"There is no time now. Zuriel, have you checked the latest intel?" The man-monster nods in response to the priest. "Well, better get cracking then."

"Indeed, Markus. Come, Ryder, let us save your damsel in distress," Zuriel says, chuckling to himself.

I see nothing amusing about the situation at all. In fact, I am still baffled and reeling from shock.

We leave via a back entrance that connects to a nearby alleyway. "Here, you drive this contraption." He points to a large van parked further up. Zuriel tosses a set of car keys towards me, but a pale hand snatches them from the air.

Sophitia dangles them from purple-painted fingernails. "I am going too. I have let you down in the past, cousin, but not now."

"What are you doing here?" I eye her warily.

She shrugs. "I followed you. Did not want you to do anything stupid."

Before I can argue, she tosses me the keys and slides into the passenger seat.

As I jump into the driver's seat, Zuriel opens the door to the back. He takes up two seats and perches forward. The man-mountain barks directions, taking us into a commercial area a few suburbs over. We stop in front of a building that reminds me of the EEF facility we broke into before Christmas, even though it is nothing like it. Yet it has the same emptiness. Like it is a shell.

"Are you sure she is here?" Sophitia asks.

From the outside it seems like nothing more than an old factory. Zuriel extends a hand between the seats and shows his handheld device. The blip on the GPS marks this as the spot.

"You implanted Mishca with a tracker?" Sophitia sounds incredulous.

"No. We made sure she was traceable. Come on." Zuriel opens the van door. He strides straight over to the building and barges into the front door with his shoulder. There is a crack of splintering wood. Alarms sound.

Not the stealthy entry I was hoping.

A team of ten guards spills forward, guns drawn.

Sophitia and I stand still in awe while Zuriel leaves half of them unconscious with some of the quickest punches I have ever seen. The remaining guards retreat inside the building. I rush forward with Zuriel, following them as they withdraw.

"Stay calm, my friends." Zuriel unbuttons his trench coat. "This is not the way I wished to introduce you to this world, but I have no choice."

He lets loose a roar and flings his coat to his ground, releasing a pair of leathery wings. I recoil. The guards do not. They firm their feet and raise their weapons. A grey tail strikes, knocking the men down. *A tail!* It sits below his wings. *What the* − This cannot be real.

Zuriel lets loose another flurry of punches, connecting with each of the remaining men. All our assailants are now unconscious, and I did not have to let loose a spark.

"My sources indicate that she could be on the lower level in a cell," Zuriel says, not meeting my stare.

I nod and we follow our companion towards the stairs. Zuriel stops short, his wings hindering him from going through the doorway. He sighs and heads back towards the fallen men to retrieve his jacket. His wings fold down as he slings it over an arm. That does not bode well. He is obviously still expecting trouble.

A cry comes from the stairwell. It is Mishca. I am sure of it. Something is terribly wrong. I race ahead, ignoring Zuriel's protests. As I stalk down the dark corridor, I feel uneasy. *Why are there no guards down here?* The walls are grey and dank. The fluorescent lights let a gentle humming resonate around me. I can hear Zuriel making his way down the stairs.

Suddenly, a sense of urgency hits me. I race to the second door on the right. Grunting from a voice that is most definitely female is muffled by the walls. It is enough to know there is a struggle, and Mishca is in danger.

I explode.

CHAPTER 29

MISHCA

THE FOG HAS STARTED TO clear, but I still feel weak and listless. A firm weight presses against my legs. I remember white-haired dude telling my guard not to hurt me when they put me in here, but he obviously didn't listen. Only five minutes after the others left, the guy watching over me says, "We are going to have a little fun."

My head feels too heavy to lift, so I listen to what's going on around me to decide on an escape route. The man in the room with me has a wheeze to his breathing and heavy footsteps. He's out of shape and more than a hundred kilos. His bad body odor supports this too. If I get my strength back in time, I can take him. But I don't have long.

Noise reaches my ears. It's happening on the levels above me—a commotion. Whatever it is it'll create a diversion and maybe I can escape.

"Ready, little lady?" the man asks, his voice rasping. "We're going to get it on."

I've got news for him. Energy returns to my limbs when he yanks my dress up to my hips. I pull my arms under my chest and push up with such force I dislodge my assailant. Springing to my feet, I whip around, pushing my left foot to the ground and my hands up with clenched fists.

My assessment was right. A stocky middle-aged man stares at me in shock. My eyes dart around the room. One closed door behind my enemy, one chair to the right—a possible weapon. Otherwise, the room is empty.

My guard recovers his wits and charges at me, his body hunched in a tackling position. I side-step his clumsy attempt and deliver a roundhouse kick to his rear, increasing the intensity of the impact between his head and the wall. He slumps to the ground with a groan.

I slip my heels off, readjust my dress, and make for the exit, then I hear yelling outside the room. How could they know that the guard is incapacitated already? My body tenses. I push my foot back and raise my knuckles, expecting to have to deal with stronger opponents than the unconscious slob on the ground.

The door bursts open. I see him. Ryder. Well, a version of him anyway. He storms in, surrounded by a circle of light that fades into a metallic blue glow. I realize his feet are not touching the ground. My gaze trails up his body, his skin shining, his blue hair. *Oh my...*

Ryder has thin membranous wings protruding from his back that seem to move effortlessly, holding him off the ground.   He cries words in a language I don't understand, his tattoos shimmering as he speaks. A long silver sword shimmers in his hand.

"Mishca!" Ryder cries, his voice lighter and more melodic than I've ever heard it.

Behind him are Sophitia and the grey-skinned man who helped us escape from the cloning facility — and they both have wings too. She glows and levitates like Ryder, but in a green hue. The man-mountain is not glowing and his feet are firmly on the ground. Ryder's sword vanishes and his color begins returning to normal. He smells like spring.

"Um, we are here to rescue you," he says uncertainly, gazing at the unconscious man on the ground.

"Reunion later." Sophitia shimmers to her regular appearance. "Right now we need to get out of here before backup arrives."

"I concur with the night elf. We must go." The grey-skinned man wraps his bat-like wings around him like a cloak, even though he holds a trench coat in his hand.

Night elf? She's a what?

Ryder encircles his hand around my wrist and pulls me towards the door. The pounding of our feet echoes through the empty corridors. Bodies are sporadically strewn across the floor that we hurdle. A heartbeat later, we arrive at a choice: an elevator or another door.

Sophitia presses the elevator button, but I peek through the other option. It's a stairwell.

"Stay here," I whisper as I reach into the elevator and push the ground floor button. It is four levels up from where we are. A strong distraction while we take the stairs. My finger presses against my lips and the others comply, treading quietly as we head up.

At the top of the stairwell, Ryder and I peer into the hallway. Two men with semi-automatic guns stare at the empty elevator. I push my boyfriend behind me and charge. My targets turn towards me too late. The first gets a fist to the jaw and goes down, unconscious. I form a fist around the barrel of the second guy's gun, yanking him towards me for a head-butt. He doubles over, clutching his head as I secure my grip on the weapon and bash it on his head.

With both of them comatose the foyer is secure. I signal to the others to move to the front door. The grey man stoops and picks a black pile on the floor. As he slings it over his shoulders and shoves his arms in I realize it's a coat. Good thing. He would attract a lot of more attention without it.

Unfortunately, in that pause the reinforcements arrive and everything goes from bad to worse. There may be thirty of them lined up with guns pointed at us. I could probably take on half of them without a sweat, but the collateral damage would be too high. No way I could guarantee the safety of my companions, no matter what they are. I raise my hands in surrender.

A green flash of light shoots across the room and the guards are frozen in place. Sweat drips from Sophitia's brow. She stands firmly in place, back in her elf form, her fingers spread and bright beams emanating from them towards the now-still men.

"Go," she yells.

The three of us are statues as though we're caught in her magic too.

"Move, now," she cries. "I cannot hold them off forever. Zuriel, you know keeping Mishca and Ryder safe is the highest priority."

"She is right. We must leave," the man-mountain says in his gravelly voice.

"No. Sophitia, you are too important to me." Ryder takes a step towards her.

"Cousin, I promised your mother I would keep you safe. For her sake, you must go." Sweat trickles down her brow.

"Not without you. I—"

A grey hand claps Ryder's shoulder. "I will make you leave by force if you make me."

Ryder and I stare at each other. We know he's not kidding after our last encounter.

"You had better be right behind us." Ryder takes three strides forward and embraces Sophitia. She grimaces but agrees.

The three of us race through the doors and into the cool air of the early morning. The sky is still inky, leaving a grey haze across everything. I turn and notice the structure, large corporate style with no branding — another faceless building in the inner city of Brisbane. I search for markers and take note it's on the corner of Westchester and Vulcan streets. After a few blocks, Ryder falls behind.

"You would be faster in your fae form," Zuriel calls over his shoulder.

Ryder clenches his jaw. "If only I knew where the

on switch was."

"How much further do we need to go?" I ask.

Ahead of us is a seemingly endless stream of tall grey buildings, the tops of which blend into the sky far above the street lights.

"Too far for them not to catch us if we keep pace with your beau. We could seek higher ground, but there is a risk of detection."

I strain to hear what is behind us and pick up the sound of a scuffle and stomping footsteps headed our way. My feet pause and I turn to Ryder.

"Hop on." I crouch down a little and lean forward.

"What?"

"You're too slow. I'm going to carry you, so hop on." Ryder doesn't move. "That's an order."

"Do as she says or Sophitia's sacrifice will be for nothing." Zuriel steps towards us like he will pick Ryder up and put him on my back himself.

For a moment Ryder stands with his fists clenched. His body twitches as though it wants to make a break from us back towards his kin. Instead, he gives us an unimpressed grimace and climbs on. I hold my shoes for him to take and then get ready to run. Zuriel reaches into his coat pocket and throws some powder in the air over us. As it settles a cold shiver trickles over me.

"It will hide us from human eyes so as not to draw attention to us," he explains. "Unfortunately, it will not stop Wirth's associates from tracking us, so we must move swiftly. Once we get to the safe house they will not be able to follow."

Zuriel and I move at a strong pace with Ryder bouncing off my hips at each stride. I clutch more firmly to his legs to minimize the movements. It feels awkward having his large frame jostling around back there, but he's not heavy and I can keep pace with Zuriel. My dress rides up and I resist the urge to pull it down, knowing that no one can see anyway.

"This seems like a poorly thought out plan, you know, having to run this far." Ryder's voice wobbles in time with the jolts of my feet pounding the pavement.

"We did have a van that was to be used," Zuriel says. "However, Sophitia has the keys. I did not realize you were unable to transform at will. Otherwise, I would have considered other options."

I readjust my grip to stop Ryder sliding off. We've moved from the commercial precinct and into an older suburb. There's no sound of footsteps behind us, which is good and bad.

"We're here." Zuriel comes to an abrupt halt in front of a run-down old Queenslander. The gate creaks and whines as he pushes it open.

Ryder slips down. "You have bony hips." His first couple of steps are like he's just gotten off a horse after a full day's ride.

"You have wings." Stating the obvious, I know.

"And you kicked major butt." He clasps my hand.

I inspect Ryder more closely and notice scrapes on his face. "You're hurt."

He shrugs. "I had an altercation with your abductors after I saw them putting you in their car.

They drove at me when I tried to stop them. It seems worse than it is."

Zuriel mutters something at the base of the stairs and motions for us to follow him. The wood groans with each step he takes. I grip Ryder's hand and march up the stairs. Inside is dark, but I can just spot minimal furniture. There's nothing in the front room but two cupboards that I suspect are an armory. We move through what should be the lounge area. A light flicks on and I'm ready for answers.

"So how did you find me?" I ask, surveying the room. Three sofas, a bookshelf, a hallway that leads to bedrooms, and internal stairs that appear to lead down to a basement.

"Your cross." My hand immediately goes to my necklace at Zuriel's words. "It has a tracker in it. Markus anticipated this might happen, which is why he gave it to you."

As creepy as the revelation is that these guys have been keeping tabs on me, there was a chance I could have been in real trouble. My body has definitely lost all the sluggishness from earlier tonight. Whatever drugs I was given won't be in my system. If they had given me more, there's no way I would have been able to rescue myself like I did. And I doubt I could've taken all those guards on.

"Stalker much? You guys have done very little that makes me want to trust you." I swallow. *Other than the fact that you're not trying to kill off my sisters.*

"I do not care if you trust me as long as you are safe." He slips off his coat and folds his leathery wings around himself.

"What about Sophitia?" Ryder cuts in.

"We wait thirty minutes, if she does not come by then we have to keep moving. I must be back at sanctuary before dawn." Zuriel shows no emotion with his words. He sits awkwardly on a blue sofa. It sags beneath his weight.

"No! We have to go back for her." Ryder paces the room like a caged lion.

I glance at the clock on the wall. "Let's discuss this after we've given her half an hour."

My words are greeted with skepticism. Zuriel doesn't expect Sophitia to make it, nor do I.

"When can we go back for her?" Ryder stops and folds his arms.

I can't bring myself to tell him about the noises I heard as we left. It sounded like she was overpowered. Instinctively, I want to case the place.

"We cannot. It's too dangerous." Zuriel grabs his discarded coat and retrieves a phone from a pocket.

"That is not good enough. She is my cousin. She knows my mother." Ryder's anger vibrates around the room.

"I'm going to check the place out," I say, expecting a protest, but the testosterone is dominating the room and it's like they don't even hear me.

No one says a word to me as I head down the hallway, past the kitchen and the bathroom. Their arguments bounce off the walls, growing fainter as I go.

The first bedroom is sparsely furnished—a bed, a

nightstand with a lamp, and nothing else. I move to the next one, which is the same. The third room has a wardrobe, a bookshelf, and desk with a computer on it.

My reflection greets me in the mirrored door as I reach to open the wardrobe. I expect to see a wide-eyed scared girl staring back; instead, there is a hardened young woman with blood splotches sprayed across her face. The blood is not mine, but that doesn't make it any easier. I match the cast member of a bad slasher flick. My blue party dress lays torn and tattered.

Swallowing hard, I slide the door open. Inside is an array of dark clothes, boots, guns, knives, and a sword. I rifle through the clothes until I find some in my size and then head to the bathroom, ignoring the growling protest from my stomach.

There's no fresh towels, but my care factor is low. I need to get clean. The showerhead hisses to life as I turn the taps. The water cascades over me and I sag against the wall. Red tainted water streams past my feet, swirling down the drain. Good scene for a horror movie.

Snatching a random towel off the rack, I dry off and slip into the borrowed clothes — a black tunic top and tight dark grey pants. I find a discarded hair-band and brush my hair into a ponytail. It'll be more comfortable to put the boots on in the lounge, so I pick them up in one hand and my trashed dress in the other.

There's no noise as I come down the hall, which could be a sign that Zuriel and Ryder have reached an agreement. The two of them are on different sides of the room, arms folded and not making eye contact with each other. Ryder flinches as he sees me, reaching for his hip like he's groping for a non-existent weapon — the sword from his fae form.

Zuriel's face tightens. "I need to go to the basement. Make sure *he* doesn't do anything stupid while I am gone."

Ryder's eyes stay on him until he's out of sight and then he turns to me. "You look so much like *her*."

My dress falls to the floor. I kick it into the corner and toss the shoes on the ground in front of me.

"Of course I do." I yank a sock on. "That's what happens with clones."

"No. I mean you seem harder, older...battle ready."

"Really?" I reply on autopilot. My eyes find the clock again. Sophitia has fifteen minutes to get here and Zuriel has forty-five minutes until he turns into a pumpkin or something.

"I could always tell you apart before. Now I am not so sure I would be able to."

My foot jams into a boot as my mind ticks over.

"I think you've just given me the answer to how we save Sophitia." I kick the boot back off. "Step one is to deal with Zuriel. There's no way he will let us go without a fight."

Ryder cocks his head as my finger finds my lips to signal for quiet and then raise my hand for him to stay put. I creep towards the stairs, treading lightly when I descend. Muffled talking slowly becomes clearer the closer I get. Zuriel has discarded his jacket, cloaking himself with his wings. Thankfully, he has his back to me.

"They want to mount a rescue effort, but I am dissuading them from the idea." The cell phone is dwarfed by his hand.

The thick metal door has multiple locks on the outside. Perfect.

The last step creaks under my foot. Zuriel turns around just as I entomb him in darkness, sliding the multiple bolts across rapidly. Fist sized dents appear as I tackle the last one.

"Mishca," Zuriel roars, almost causing my hands to slip off the padlock. "Release me at once."

CHAPTER 30

RYDER

"WHAT ARE YOU DOING?" I ask from the top of the stairs.

"Making sure we can get Sophitia back." The fastened metal lock clangs against the door as Mishca lets it drop. "There's no way *he'd* let us go through with my plan. Chances are he'd herd us back to the priest and we'd be even further away from her." She glances at me skeptically.

I involuntarily cringe at the continued yelling and banging. Mishca walks back upstairs and leads us to the main bedroom. She sits at a desk and fires up the computer.

"I am assuming you have a plan?" I sit on the bed behind her.

"We need to get ourselves ready. We can't barge in. Sustenance is important. We need energy to fight." She sounds so matter-of-fact. "So breakfast and planning. We have to get this right. But first we should do some research, about you and Sophitia. What has she told you so far?"

"She was not overly forthcoming with information. We are both fae, which I realized myself when I sprouted wings, and we are related, cousins. My mother asked her to watch over me, but she would not give me any details. Zuriel called her a night elf, so maybe I am one too."

The glowing computer screen snags our attention.

"Okay, let's see." She reads over the website. "Fae are often elemental, which explains the lightning. You're good with magic and weapon making."

Searching for *lightning fae* and *night elf* brings up a whole bunch of stuff that would have a Dungeons and Dragons enthusiast drooling.

"Good news, you're invulnerable to poison and heal super quickly. Bad news, you're allergic to iron and lemon juice and you're easily distracted by shiny things. *And* you can die of a broken heart." She points at the list on the screen.

"Stay with me and we will be fine then," I quip.

"Apparently, fae like to steal people too. Not nice."

I raise my hands defensively.

There is very little on night elves, apart from gaming information. As she changes the words to *fae change*, the search suggests *changeling*, which she ignores and continues with her search.

"Here." She gestures to the new page.

I read over her shoulder. The first post includes fae glamours, but only mentions it briefly. She opens up a new site with more detail.

"Do you think this is what you're doing?

Subconsciously using a glamour?" she asks.

"I am not sure."

"Well if you are, then you're rare," she says as she speed-reads through the content. "Most fae can only hold a glamour for an hour or so. And guess what else?"

"What?" I skim over the screen.

"Legend has it fairies are grammar nerds who don't like to use contractions." She pokes her tongue at me.

I frown. "As interesting as that is, how does it help us for rescuing Sophitia?"

She sighs and pushes the chair away from the desk. "Nothing really. There's too much information and no telling what's real and what's myth. Some say you guys are great at making weapons, and others say it hurts you just to be around iron. But I think that's a myth, or out-of-date, or something."

"So what next?" I wince as a fresh round of yelling starts up from the basement.

"In a minute, breakfast. But first I need to check something."

With a few clicks the fake Michelle Facebook account pops up. Andrea has accepted the friend request and left a message.

*Squee! So excited that you found me. I think we might be related. I saw you in the paper and we look so much alike *points to profile pic*. I've been searching for my birth family (yeah, I'm adopted), but I haven't had much luck making contact. Then, there you were in the paper looking just like me. I live about an hour away from you in Airlie Beach, but I'm away on holidays with my family overseas at the* *moment. Please reply so we can get catch up when I get back. <3 Andrea.*

"This seemed like a good idea at the time, but what do I say now?"

I shrug.

Mishca begins to type.

I'm not Michelle, 'cause our other sister killed her and you are next on the list. By the way, we're clones.

"Nope, that's not going to work. Tammy has a pretty wild imagination. Her automatic reaction was for something outrageous, though the truth was beyond her concept of reality. But she could see the truth on my face." She holds down the delete button.

"Go for a modified version of the truth," I say, wanting to be helpful.

Hey Andrea, I'm so excited we caught up. But I'm scared too. I tracked you down and went to visit you at your home. There was someone there and I overheard them saying they're going to kill you! It was a bit freaky and I got out of there. Stay away and stay safe.

"It's the truth without telling her everything. With luck, she'll show her parents and they'll check in at home to discover the signs of a fight at their house and take heed of the warning. Not much weight in the words of a stranger behind a Facebook profile."

I read over her shoulder. "Not sure that will work."

"Me neither." She says and presses send anyway. "Better than nothing."

Mishca logs off from the fake account and into her actual Facebook account. "My phone went missing somewhere in the scuffle at The Bowl, so I'll take the opportunity to message Nerissa and let her know I'm okay." Her stomach gives a growl. She ignores it until she has finished the message to Nerissa. "Let's inspect the rations."

Zuriel's protests grow louder as we go towards the kitchen. But Mishca continues through to the front room and peers between curtains.

"Double checking we weren't followed." She volunteers the information even though I never asked.

I lift part of the material away as well. No one suspicious is in sight, only dark shadows of buildings against the hazy lightening sky. The first ray of sunshine streams in through the curtain, revealing speckles of dust dancing in the beam. Not much housework been done here recently. It is oddly calming. Even the man-mountain downstairs must feel it as he has gone silent too.

We retreat to the kitchen, my stomach making as much noise as Mishca's. I open up the fridge. There is not much, but enough.

"Found eggs." I hold up a carton in triumph.

Mishca roots through the cupboards and claims a pot. She hands them to me, checks the freezer, and retrieves half a loaf of bread. She plonks two pieces in the toaster and shoves the lever down. I open more doors and find some plates and knives. I set the table, sit down, and stare at Mishca.

"So, you said you have found the answer? What is it?"

"We go back in, this morning, as soon as we've eaten." She goes to the fridge and returns with butter.

"You think we are going to be able to simply walk into the building and rescue Sophitia?"

"Yep." She gives me a sneaky smirk.

"And how are we going to manage that?" I run a hand through my hair.

"Well, I'm going to go in there and take her."

The toast pops up behind me. Then, the sound of a knife scraping across the brown surface is the only noise in the room.

"No." My chair squeals in protest as I push it back across the cool lino floor. I place clenched knuckles on the table.

"Yes. You heard Zuriel. You're important too. It has to be me. I'm the only one who can do it." She places a plate with buttered toast in front of me like our debate isn't even happening.

"The moment they see you, they will take you prisoner again. The four of us were not enough to overpower them last night. And you want me to let you go in by yourself? I am coming too."

Her eyebrows shoot up at "let."

The timer beeps for the eggs. She snags the pot off the stove and tips the hot water out, careful to put it against the side of the sink so the eggs do not escape, and then fills it with cold water.

"Not with what I've got planned. Brute force isn't the way to get Sophitia back. You said so yourself, it didn't work. If we go in all guns blazing, it won't work. But deception and stealth will."

"So what have you got planned?"

"I'm going to walk in the front door, head high,

sneer on my face, just like her."

"Her? You think you can pass for…"

She nods. "That's exactly what I'm thinking."

CHAPTER 31

MISHCA

THE BASEMENT REMAINS eerily quiet. Zuriel made such a racket for the first half an hour of his imprisonment, but he hasn't made a sound for the past six hours. My feet don't want to move from the top of the stairs in case he's faking. I half expect him to burst through the door at any moment. No, it's better I stay here with an easy escape route.

"Zuriel?" My voice isn't as firm and authoritative as I want it to be, as I need it to be. Silence. "I'm going back in as Othilia. It's our best chance to get Sophitia."

Ryder steps closer to me. "Are you sure this is a good idea? What if Othilia is there?"

I don't know if he's referring to my attempts to engage Zuriel or the rescue attempt. Either way, I ignore it.

"Is there anything that you can tell me about the compound? Anything I need to know?" I call to Zuriel, sterner than before, more like *her*. But not close enough.

There's still no answer and there's no point in

prolonging my leaving any longer. All morning we've researched the area through aerial maps, hacked into local security systems — thanks to Connor remote accessing in. There's been no sign of Othilia on site. I can only hope she doesn't come in, or else the plan will bomb. The guards are about the area, but there's fewer of them than last night. Probably because a day siege isn't a logical strategy. It's our advantage, our edge. I don't want to wait any longer.

Spinning on my heels, I walk with determination to the front room to investigate the contents of the cupboards. I hadn't noticed the locks last night, but it doesn't matter. My hand grips the first padlock and I yank hard. The latch gives and the door swings loosely. Inside are weapons. I pick a knife and a small handgun, both easily concealable. The blade goes in my right boot. For the gun, I strip off my jacket and put on a small holster that straps around my back and arms. The leather carrier sits beside my breast. The rest of the contents are only good for storming the castle, so to speak.

The next cupboard opens as easily, but the booty inside is decidedly different: trackers, tiny earpiece communiqués, and a whole heap of surveillance equipment. I wish I had known about all this last night as I could have done a proper perimeter sweep and a stakeout. I rifle through, find two small earpieces, and hand one to Ryder.

"Here, this way we can stay in contact. Put it in your ear," I say, putting mine in, "and we will have comms. They're already tuned to the same frequency, so don't muck about with that. They're short range though, so we're going to have to find somewhere for you to hole up."

"There was a café two blocks up." He nods. "It was on Westchester."

"Sounds good." I make a move for the door, but Ryder heads into the lounge.

"Hang on," he calls from the next room. He returns with a book on mythology. "I found it on the bookshelf in the other room. So I've got a reason to hang around the café for so long."

"Good idea."

Ryder and I are channelling a couple of wannabe emos, all dressed in black minus the makeup. It's going to be an hour walk. Normally, I'd love an hour together, strolling through the city. Not today. We have to remain apart. Chances are they'll be expecting us to be together. It's easier to be under the radar separately.

I get Ryder to walk two blocks ahead of me. Even in the lunchtime rush, I can easily pick him in the crowd if I need to get to him quickly. The last thing I want is him going all fae if he sees me in any perceived danger. The whole time my eyes flick around, trying to identify any of the guards from last night, Othilia, and the man with the white hair who took me from the club. Any of them could blow my cover.

Despite having to weave between corporate suits that cover the streets like ants at a picnic, we make good time. Ryder peels off and takes a seat at the café. I move on without a sideways glance.

"Good luck," says his soft voice in my ear.

I let a smile take over my lips and then frown. *She* wouldn't smile like that in the street.

My head stays high, purposeful as I cross the street into the faceless building, hiding in plain sight, not pretending to be anything else. On the same block is a government building, an insurance agency, and a bank.

There's nothing but the entrance. I push the doors and see two guards jump to attention, guns raised. A black-haired secretary picks up a phone.

"Stand down, morons," I snarl in a manner I've heard my sister use before. "It's me."

"Sorry, ma'am," stammers one, holstering his weapon. "I thought you were part of the interrogation team. I wasn't expecting to see you here."

I stare at the receptionist until she puts the phone handle back down. "So you thought a more logical option was for that stray to waltz right in through the front door." I sneer. Mental note—Othilia is at an interrogation that sounds like it's off site. Good, she shouldn't be coming in then. As long as it's not Sophitia she's questioning, or else we're boned.

"I guess not."

"Idiot," I add for good measure and then head for the stairwell that leads to the basement. My boots click on the white tiles. It's quite a nice foyer, something I wasn't able to take in when we were being cornered by thirty guards.

I hurry to the lower level where the prisoners are kept. I don't recall there being any inmates with me, so I'm hoping it's only Sophitia down there. The moment I reach the right floor, I realize I won't be alone. There's a moving shadow on the other side of the door.

Gripping the handle, I take a deep breath and push. A startled sentry on the other side relaxes when he sees me.

"Othilia. I was not expecting you."

"I need to see the prisoner," I snap, praying that my sister is as much of a bitch to everyone else as she is to me.

"Haven't you heard? She escaped." The sentry's voice trembles as though he doesn't want to be the one delivering the news.

"Sophitia escaped?" I reply in shock. I'm in the den of the lion for nothing.

A wave of confusion washing over his face. "The green-haired one? She is up on level five."

"Thanks." I turn sharply and head straight back into the stairwell.

When I'm out of sight I fall against the wall and catch my breath. Maybe that's where the interrogation is. My feet are light and cautious heading up the stairs. I need to be on alert for Othilia. I pause at the door at level two, feeling a pull. Before I can stop myself, I'm gripping the handle and through the door.

The walls are white and the glare from the sun streaming in through the large windows makes me need to shield my eyes. There's a muffled conversation behind the door at the end of the room. Blast not having x-ray vision. I creep closer. My breath catches in my throat at the mention of a name, "Wirth." He's not being spoken about, but spoken to. I move quicker this time and hover outside the room.

I press my cheek against the door. Behind there is the man who created me. A yearning to open the door pulls at my being, to see the man who created me, the man who ordered the death of his children. Did he feel any pain over it? I could pull the blade from my boot and stab him through the heart, or grab my gun and shoot him between the eyes. Surprisingly, neither image gives me any satisfaction. I place my hand against the door, pushing back, resisting the crazy-ass urge I'm feeling to rush to my father.

Soldier. What is your malfunction? This is not the mission. I wrench away and withdraw to the stairwell, trembling. Father? How could I even think that?

If Wirth has that effect on me just from being in the same building, how will I cope with it if I come face-to-face with him?

I march up the rest of the stairs until I reach floor five. Willing my senses to full capacity, I search for my sister, but there's nothing. There's no sound of anyone else in the hallway either. I make my move. I pause and listen for Sophitia.

"I cannot tell you that." Her voice rings out to me from a room at the end of the corridor.

Two guards come from a different room and head towards the elevators at the center of the corridor. I walk to them, doing my best to put on an air of confidence. They nod at me, stopping at the elevator door. I hold my breath until the ping for the door opening sounds, followed by the sliding *whoosh* of them closing again.

"Othilia?"

Oh shit. I spin and see the barman from The Bowl, his blue eyes pierce through me.

"What do you want, idiot?" I snap, hoping Othilia is as rude as I think she is. My legs break into a fast trot down the hall past him.

"Now, now. That is no way to address royalty," he says, sounding serious. But the corner of his mouth quirks.

"I'm so sorry, your highness." I turn and give a mocking courtesy.

"That is better." He advances towards me, a leer crossing his face.

My eyes shift around, searching for an exit. There's something in his eyes that makes my gut churn.

"You know what I really like?" he whispers as he stands right in front of me. Strong hands encircle my throat while his breath hits my ear. "I love it when you say my name."

As I reach to throw him off me, he nuzzles my ear, kissing down my face. "I have missed you, Othilia. Say my name."

My body stiffens. His mouth finds mine. He pulls back.

"You are not—"

I strike my knee into his groin and then twist my arms around his neck as he doubles over. Using his head like a battering ram, I drive him repeatedly into the wall until blood drips across the floor. I toss him like a ragdoll. Red seeps over his forehead, tinging his hair with pink.

Crouching next to his prone body, I examine him.

His features flicker. His skin goes from tanned to pale white where his ears extend. The blood slows and the gash closes. His eyes flicker purple. He's fae! And he's not on our side.

"Oh sh-"

Purple wings extended, the fae barman springs at me. I sidestep easily, causing him to yell.

"Adair, is everything alright?" A guard pokes his head from a room. Inside Sophitia in her human façade stares back at me wide-eyed.

"Of course not," Adair screams. "Get her."

The guard twists towards me, pulling his gun. My body contorts as bullets fly past, one grazing my leg. The heel of my palm crushes his jaw, driving his head against the wall. The impact leaves him like a coma patient.

A sword shrouded in black flames gleams in Adair's hand. The wind whistles as he strikes it at me.

"No," Sophitia yells, moving between us.

The sword slices into her arm. Her skin sizzles. She grips the weapon, blood oozing through her fingers, and grimaces.

Adair laughs. "Really, Sophitia. You would put yourself in harm's way for a *human?*"

Instead of responding, she whispers some words and the air ripples around us. He slices at us again, but his sword stops mid-air like it hit something. Adair pushes, sweating under the strain. But the sword holds still.

"Guards to level five," Adair calls into a two-way he pulls from his pocket. "I am betting your protection spell only works against magical weapons. Let us test it against bullets."

"Now would be a good time to sprout wings," I yell as I tackle Sophitia and slam the two of us through a window.

Glass shatters all around us. Tiny splinters pierce my skin. My companion swears. I grimace, but can't worry about that as the ground quickly comes towards us. Sophitia's skin shimmers green. Her wings push against my arms, but I can't loosen my grip to let them free. My fingers heat up. *Great plan, Mishca.* I twist and take the full force of both our weight as we hit the ground.

I groan and push Sophitia off me. She appears winded, but unharmed further. Her arm hasn't healed instantly like Adair's forehead, but it's no longer bleeding.

"Are you crazy?" Sophitia gives a shiver and then transforms back to normal. Luckily, we landed in an alleyway and not on the main street. "You should not have come for me."

"Ryder needs you. I had no choice." I press against the earpiece. "I've got her, keep your eyes peeled for us."

"Roger that," comes Ryder's crackly voice in my ear.

She glances up. Adair leans through the window scowling. From behind him comes yelling, and lots of it.

"This way." Sophitia points to her left. She doesn't sound happy to see me.

We head for the road. She whispers some words and the air around us seems to shiver. Everyone we run past is oblivious to us.

CHAPTER 32

RYDER

"I'VE GOT HER, keep your eyes peeled for us." Mishca's voice finally comes through. For the past twenty minutes I have been going out of my mind.

"Roger that." I let go of my earpiece to cut communication.

I scan the streets, but see nothing. They should be in view. Then, I shiver and Mishca and Sophitia appear before me.

I have an urge to hug them both at once, but stay still.

"Come on," Mishca says in a low voice. "We need to keep going."

We jog for another block until Sophitia commands us to stop. "We are at the van." She points to a nearby alley.

The three of us pile in with me driving. I readjust the mirror and get the view of the back of Mishca's head as she gazes through the rear window.

"You two are the biggest idiots I have ever met. If

your mother knew the danger you put yourself in...And Mishca! Markus would kick your arse if he knew you virtually gift wrapped yourself for Wirth."

"How about 'thanks, Mishca and Ryder, for saving my butt.'" Mishca sounds way too much like Othilia. Her head doesn't turn around. No doubt she is searching for tails.

"Gee. Thank you, Lord and Lady of Stupidity, for risking your precious butts for my unimportant one."

"Did your research bring up any notes on fae sarcasm?" Mishca asks, just as sarcastically.

Sophitia sighs. "Yes, I am grateful. But you risked too much."

We pull up to the Queenslander. The three of us hurry from the van. Sophitia knows the words and we are quickly through the wards and upstairs.

Mishca and I head down to the basement while Sophitia goes into the kitchen.

"Zuriel," I call. "We are back."

No response.

Mishca tries. "I'm not unlocking these doors until I know you'll behave when you get free." Still nothing. "Well, fuck you."

We trudge upstairs. Sophitia sits in silence at the table, eyeing us warily. We join her. Mishca locks her fingers together in front of her and twiddles her thumbs.

"Where to start?" Mishca says. Then, she blurts out. "So, you're both elves?"

I give Sophitia a sideways glance, unsure of her reaction.

"No," she replies. "I am the offspring of an elf and a dark fae, which makes me a night elf. Ryder, you are full fae, or fairy as you may know them — close kin, easily mistaken as the same to the untrained eye."

"And you knew about me before tonight?" Mishca asks.

She nods. "I was commissioned to watch over you."

"By who?" Mishca raises a brow.

"I cannot say," she says with conviction.

"Bullshit." I am so frustrated with her acting like an enigma.

"No, I literally cannot say. I have a binding spell on me and fae are unable to lie."

"I think she's telling the truth." Mishca cracks her knuckles absentmindedly. "I vaguely remember reading that in a novel. It also included they are good at twisting the truth."

"So what can you tell us?" I stand up and shove my hands into my jeans' pockets.

"That you needed to be kept secure and hidden in such a way that it did not even appear like you were gone. It had worked well until tonight. No doubt there will be questions about the unregistered fairy in Wirth's facility."

"Anything else?" Mishca prods.

"Do not let iron pierce your skin. It is instant death. Humans should never eat our food. Fae do not use contractions." The corners of her mouth twitches with amusement. "And your family loves you very much."

I sit back down and sigh.

"What about me?" Mishca taps the table. "Did you

know about me? You know about Wirth."

Sophitia nods. "Yes. We were aware of Wirth's activities. When I saw you, I knew you were one of his."

"Did you know my mother?" Mishca tries to glean more information on Imogene, her original. But Sophitia doesn't know. "Then how did you know I was one of his clones?"

"I could sense the two of you together in one body. Traces of your mother, as you call her, linger within you. You can never be wholly apart from her, and at the same time, never truly identical to her as you have experienced a different life than her."

The silence carries on a moment before Sophitia continues. "After our first encounter, I checked with my sources and they confirmed my suspicions of your origins. I had heard of the replicas before, and I have seen beings occupy other identities, but I had never met a being with two life essences in them before I met you. It fascinated me — and it still does." This time she does smile.

"Can you tell me about your life with the fae?" I ask, changing the subject.

Sophitia laughs. "You have the fairy cunning. That question should indeed be a way for me to divulge more under normal circumstances. But this binding spell on me prevents those topics also."

An "oh" escapes Mishca's lips.

"There'd better not be one on Markus," Mishca says, "because I don't think I could be as calm as you faced with a lack of answers."

"Where is Zuriel?" Sophitia asks, a high level of caution in her voice.

"In the basement." Mishca motions toward the stairs. "He hasn't said a word to us since dawn. I told him I won't open the door until he behaves."

Sophitia stands. "He will be fine in there for a few more hours, until the sun sets. Come. Although I am limited in what I can say, there is nothing preventing me from showing you the library."

We follow her to a back room with the computer. I never even bothered to peruse the bookshelf. She picks up a book and tosses it over to us. *Fae Mythology: Truth and Fiction* is emblazed in gold. There is a ton of other books on mythical creatures and objects. I scan through the titles when a phone rings in Sophitia's pocket.

She answers it, leaving the room and heading towards the front of the house.

"Crap. I left that other book at the café."

"It should be fine." Mishca flips through the pages of the large volume.

I open my mouth but she puts a finger to my lips.

"She is saying something did not go to plan." Mishca cocks her head to the side. "The other person is laughing, but I can't make out anything more. They're words are too muffled."

Another pause. "She's coming back."

Mishca pulls me onto the bed. I act oh so nonchalant, wishing I could be as stone-cold as Mishca. But then again, no. I would never want to be as devoid of emotion as she appears right now. The bed is still bouncing slightly as Sophitia comes in.

"Find anything interesting?" she asks.

"We can hold glamours for much longer than the website said," I say, my nose in the book on a random page.

"Keep going. There is much more." Her eyes seem to twinkle in screen light.

"We should probably get going." Mishca waves at the door. "I didn't make it home last night and my parents will be freaking."

"Take it with you." Sophitia picks up another book. "And this one too."

The phone in her pocket beeps again. She pulls it free and frowns as she reads the message.

"Call this number." She tosses the phone to Mishca.

Mishca catches it in one hand and reads the message. Her fingers find the numbers and she puts the phone to her ear.

"Hello."

She recoils and leaves the room. The conversation is short. She wanders back into the room, looking like a newly turned zombie.

"We have to go." Color creeps back to her face.

"Are you okay?" I close the book.

She nods and shakes like she's doing a dance from the Wiggles before handing the phone to Sophitia.

I glance at my cousin. "Will you be alright with Zuriel, cousin?"

"I will care for him. You get yourselves home. I am sure Markus has arranged for wards on both your houses by now."

"Will we need any passwords like here?" I ask.

"No, otherwise he would have to alert Mishca's parents to the danger. Go home and rest. Then, tomorrow go to the church and see Markus."

CHAPTER 33

MISHCA

"WELL, MISHCA, YOU HAVE responded to the treatment better than anyone I have seen before. All signs point to your body fully accepting your new heart. You'll have to come back for an annual biopsy still, but keep up your meds and you can live a normal life."

I hold back a sardonic smile. A normal life, if only that was an option.

Being a genetically modified super soldier with a fae boyfriend caught in the middle of an impending war…a normal life sounds nice right about now.

Mum gives my leg a little squeeze. "That's such great news, honey."

"Perfect for you getting back into uni." Dad's grin is bigger than when the Barbarians have a win.

Uni. It should be some of the best years of my life, but I'll spend it glancing over my shoulder. A pang of guilt sinks like a stone in my stomach. Until we can discover more, Tammy has to stay at Fin's, hidden from view. But she's safe, and that's what matters.

I zone out as the doctor and my parents talk more about what I need to do from here. Inside, I know there's nothing wrong with my heart now. Whether it was from being accidently activated or when I interfaced with the computer, I'm not sure. "You have a good time with the rest of your life, Mishca."

"Huh?" My head snaps back to Dr. Thompson.

"I said have a great life," he repeats with warmth in his voice.

"ACK," I say, thinking about what I've got to do after this appointment. When everyone else looks at me like I just said I wanted to be a stripper on Mars for using military speech for "acknowledge" I add, "Ah, sure."

Mum and Dad hold hands as we leave the office. Ryder is in the waiting room, seeming uncomfortable on the hard plastic chair. We got read the riot act by my folks. I'm sure they wish they could ground me.

"How did it go?" he asks hesitantly.

"Everything's great." Mum beams. "Mishca can do all the same things as a regular teenage girl now, according to Dr. Thompson."

Dad pulls Mum and me into a hug. "Alright, we'd better let these two lovebirds get on with their date. But be home *on time*."

"Yes, have fun you two." Mum's grin would put the Cheshire Cat to shame.

Dad raises an eyebrow and stares at Ryder. "But not too much fun."

"Yes, sir." Ryder sounds like he should be saluting.

I seize my boyfriend's hand and pull him away with a goodbye wave to my parents.

As we make our way down the white corridor he asks, "Are you sure you're ready for this?"

"Yep. I've got to know. And so does Tammy." I give his hand a little squeeze as I answer.

The glare from the sun is so bright when we leave the hospital that I have to shelter my eyes. I scan the parking lot for Ryder's car. I haven't felt Othilia since we got back.

"Do you really think Markus and Zuriel are going to have answers?" Ryder climbs into the driver's side. "So far they have us running around in circles."

"It's worth a try." I follow him in.

I chew my fingernails on the ride over to the church, staring at the scenery that flashes past. Houses, shops, and cars flash by, but none of them catch my attention until we reach The Bowl. Then, I know we're only a couple of blocks away.

We pull in across the street and get out of the car. We're about to cross the road when I pull up short and grip Ryder's arm.

"There." I point up.

At the top of the building, nestled amongst smaller gargoyle statues, is Zuriel, frozen in stone. It's weird to see him as an adornment on the rooftop.

"Wow, he really is a..." My voice trails off.

Ryder grunts. "I did not believe in fairies a few weeks ago. But it is hard not to believe in one's self. Who knows what else exists."

"But a real gargoyle?" I keep my eyes on stone

Zuriel while we make our way.

"It would explain a lot. He was so strong, and big, and grey." Ryder crosses his eyes and pulls a face.

I laugh, appreciating his attempt to lighten the situation. He's coped with his out-of-left-field news better than I did. No shame spiral, just more determination to meet his birth mother and get answers.

The front door creaks in protest when I push it. The tingling tells me what I need to know. In the pews at the front of the church, Tammy and Fin are waiting. She's safe. My sister and I rush to each other and embrace.

"I've missed you," I whisper. For some reason I feel less empty when she's around.

"Me too," she says into my hair.

Nerissa wanted to come, but I need to keep her as far away from these people as possible. No need for her to be in the line of danger.

"Did you notice the roof, bro?" Fin asks, his eyes gesturing skyward.

"Sure did." Ryder's lips thin.

"Tempted to go up there with a baseball bat for knocking us out at EEFS, but you know, he helped you save Mishca." Fin cracks his knuckles as though he's still contemplating some payback.

A man clears his voice from behind us. Our heads all whip around to see Markus, decked in priest garb, coming from his back room. He's flanked by a small group of people I don't know with the exception of Sophitia. They're all dressed in black military style clothes. Four guys, two girls. I don't tingle at any of them.

"I see you had a fruitful trip to Townsville. Hello, Tammy. It's so nice to meet you." Markus holds his arm to my sister and they shake hands. "I'm so sorry about Michelle. Very regrettable."

"What about me?" Fin's eyebrows pinch together. "You going to give me some pearls of wisdom?"

"I'm sorry." Markus cocks his head as he studies Fin. "I don't know who you — oh, I see. I wasn't aware of you. Your father was meant to have been made sterile as part of the experiment."

Fin clenches his fists and his face contorts in anger. A couple of the guys in the group tense up, but Sophitia holds her hand up and they relax.

"Not *my* experiments," Markus hastens to add. "These are things I've learned."

"So who are you?" Tammy asks.

"Please sit." Markus gestures to the pews.

We all oblige his request. I clasp Ryder's hands with mine, worried about what will come next, but eager at the same time to know more. My eyes dart back to the group behind the priest, watching for any sudden movements or suspicious behavior.

"I am a servant of The Church and it is my job to watch for unnatural breaches between different dimensions that could jeopardize Earth — whether it's the fae realm or Hell. If any threat arises, I'm to nullify it." Markus clears his throat. "Mishca, seeing as you know you are a clone, I assume you know about Wirth."

"Yes." I struggle to meet his gaze. It's daunting for a stranger to know something so intimate about me. "He created me and Tammy and had something to do with cloning Finlay's dad. I know we're meant to be soldiers, but I don't know what we were created to fight for."

No one flinches at my words. I narrow my eyes, scrutinizing Markus' face, but he gives nothing away.

"That's about right," the priest says. "There is a portal that Wirth found out about that he believes will bring him eternal life. Nothing I've read shows that these beliefs are grounded in any form of reality. The portal is actually a pathway to Hell. Opening it would release unthinkable evil onto the world."

I gasp.

"The Church protects it well, and Wirth was unable to penetrate our defenses. So he started amassing an army to take the portal by force. The time for watching has passed. And the time for negotiations have passed. Many agents of the Church have tried to convince him of the danger, but he doesn't believe us. I have been tasked with putting together our own army to combat Wirth's and I would like you all to join us." Markus extends his arm and makes a sweeping motion. "All of you."

No one speaks.

"The Church may not seem current or cool to you, but there have always been light legions to fight the dark. And it's still my duty to keep the world safe."

The four of us take sideways glances at each other. *Is this guy for real?* I thought I would have been created to overthrow a nation, to be a part of a terrorist cell, or even to be in the service of a criminal mastermind stealing treasure. But some creeper's crazy quest for eternal life? This is beyond surreal. Now I'm expected to take sides. I slouch back in my chair, letting it all sink in.

"That's jacked up," Fin says, finally breaking the silence. "You expect us to believe you?"

"Do we have a choice?" I cut in.

"Of course, I'm pretty big on the whole 'free will' concept," the priest says.

"But you are still making it one side or the other. What if we choose to be Switzerland on this?" Ryder asks.

"That's your choice. The threat is real and coming whether you join with me or not. But if you don't join with me, I can't protect you. Wirth will want Mishca and Tammy, and you as well, Finlay, if he finds out about you." Markus runs a hand through his hair.

I suck on my bottom lip as questions race through my mind. There's a lot to weigh up.

Tammy beats me to it. "I've got questions."

"Me too," I say. I'm really concerned Tammy was so quick to ask questions. She doesn't have any of my enhancements activated. She shouldn't be joining the fight.

"Where would we live?" Tammy purposely faces away from me.

"You could stay with Zuriel and me here to avoid detection. Everyone else could stay at home," Markus stares at us intently, "for now anyway."

"But Tammy isn't like me, what use is she to you?" It's my turn to shift my gaze away.

The priest cocks an eyebrow. "That would depend on Tammy. I can activate her, or —"

"And set off the control program?" I have to work hard to stop my voice from rising to a shriek.

"No. I can stop that," Markus says.

"Really?" I can't hide the skepticism in my voice.

"Yes. I can do it for you too."

"Even if she does not want to join you?" Ryder asks.

Markus nods. "Give me a minute."

He goes briefly into the back room and returns with a bottle of pills. He hands them to me.

"Take these each night before sleep and keep a dream journal. Once you've gone a week without the dreams about guilt and lack of self-worth, stop taking the pills." Markus pauses and then continues answering my initial question, "Or Tammy can stay deactivated and train in a noncombat capacity. Either way, we'll equip her to defend herself."

I rattle the bottle of pills back and forth, letting the contents trickle while I weigh the options. I glance at Tammy. She's chewing on her fingernails. But she nods at me, and I know we both will do what we have to, even if it's not the same thing. My heart hammers in my chest. On one hand, it would be good to get payback on those responsible for tearing my life apart. But I don't fully trust Markus or the group behind him. He knew about me when I came to him in anguish, and he never revealed himself or his knowledge. That's like lying in my books.

My overriding thought? Either way I'm going to be used. After escaping, Wirth might decide one clone isn't worth the trouble. He had a hundred or so growing in the facility, and who knows how many other sleeper soldiers exist, like the clones of Fin's dad.

Tammy's eyes are now clear of tears, replaced instead with a steely determination. And in that instant I know what she's going to do.

"I'll join with you." Tammy rises to her feet. "I'm sorry, Mishca. I'm not trying to force you to go one way or the other, but until Wirth is dealt with I can't go home and I can't live in peace. I don't want to hide at Fin's for the rest of my life."

"It's okay. I understand. I'm not on their hit list." I mean the words, but the sting ring of hollow disappointment.

"Yeah," Ryder says. "You are just on their kidnap-and-turn-into-a-killing-machine list."

Fin snorts.

"I want you to be safe and if he can do that," I gesture to Markus, "then that's what you need to do."

I can't protect her and it eats me up inside. If she were like me, she'd be safe. Well, safer.

Tammy gives me a hug. "Thanks for understanding, sis."

Images of my parents cloud my mind. The happy times, watching Dad training at the football grounds, helping Mum pick an outfit before going to lunch, the three of us swimming in the pool. It gets overtaken by images of future battles where I'm required to kill Othilia, Finlay's dad, and other innocents who happened to grow in Wirth's test tubes. I release my sister and turn to Markus.

"It's too much to ask. I'm glad you can keep Tammy safe, but I want a normal life, nothing more." Doubt invades me as the words leave my mouth. I feel like such a coward, but it's not fear that's driven my decision.

"This is not our fight." Ryder stands closer to me.

"I understand why you feel that way. I hope you will reconsider as this is what you were created to do." Markus keeps his palms out as though that will placate me.

"No, it's not." I stare Markus square in the eyes. "I was created to defeat you, not fight *with* you."

"Touché." Markus tips his head towards me. "But contact me if you change your mind, because believe me, Wirth doesn't share my views on freedom of choice."

"I'll keep that in mind." My tone is cooler than I intended. I don't appreciate being cornered, or the scowls that are developing behind Markus.

"I don't know about you guys, but I've heard enough." Fin turns towards the door.

"Take care." I embrace Tammy as though we might never see each other again. Once I release her I turn to Markus. "You know what I'm capable of. I will hunt you down if you're lying and you hurt her."

Markus nods. "Of course."

"Can I still visit her?" I ask, a bit embarrassed at how harsh I had been.

"Yes." Markus folds his arms and clasps a hand

over his other wrist. "But you need to let me know before you come. You still have my card?"

Ryder nods. "Yes, I have it."

"Good." Markus gives a sad smile. "Take care and God bless. The door is always open to you if you change your mind or need refuge."

I join Ryder and Fin as they stalk from the church. Only I turn to get a final glimpse of Tammy. We both have tears in our eyes. Even though I've chosen to be neutral, I still feel like we're on opposite sides. From the way her face droops, she feels the same way.

Outside the sun is still shining brightly. I pause, close my eyes, and inhale, letting the rays warm my face. Ryder slips his hand into mine. In that instant everything is normal, like it was when we first met. My hand clenches the bottle from Markus; it's my chance to erase the reminder that I'm not a normal girl about to go to university. It represents the end of a chapter of my life. But I know it's really a beginning.

EPILOGUE

MISHCA

THE NIGHT IS COOL for summer. A light breeze plays with leaves on our back patio, tossing them into the air before letting them fall again. I sit and wait. The house behind me is still and empty. Getting my parents to leave the house was easy; keeping my nerves steady is not.

The sound of leathery wings cuts through the air and my house shudders as Zuriel lands beside the pool with Markus in his arms. He puts the priest down, folds his wings around himself, and steps back into the shadow.

I get to my feet and hug myself as I shiver. "Did it work?"

"Yes, they all believe you haven't joined us."

"Why is he here?" I gesture to Zuriel, who grunts at my words. "I thought you didn't know who the mole was."

Markus shakes his head. "I trust Zuriel absolutely. If it makes you feel any better, the information leakage happened during the day."

"Is Tammy okay?"

"She's fine." Markus places his palm on his heart. "We will keep her as safe as we can."

"So what now?" I look past him at Zuriel, who is so still he could pass for his statue form.

"You wait, behave like everything is normal. That should keep your family safe. If Wirth thinks you have rejected my offer, then he should be in no rush to rein you in. He'll call you for duty when he's getting ready to strike. But by then we'll have made our move."

"I'll be ready." I stand a bit taller.

"I know," he replies.

We grip each other's hands to confirm our new alliance then he strides back to Zuriel. The man-giant scoops him up and then jumps off the edge, wings extended.

The deception was necessary, yet it sits uncomfortably with me. But I'm ready to take it to my maker. I'm ready to fight.

THE END

Thank you for reading! Find book three in the Open Heart series featuring new mysteries and thrills for Mishca, Ryder, and friends in 2017!

Please sign up for the City Owl Press newsletter for chances to win special subscriber-only contests and giveaways as well as receiving information on upcoming releases and special excerpts.

www.sharonmjohnston.com
@S_M_Johnston

All reviews are welcome and appreciated. Please consider leaving one on your favorite social media and book buying sites.

For books in the world of romance and speculative fiction that embody Innovation, Creativity, and Affordability, check out City Owl Press at www.cityowlpress.com.

ACKNOWLEDGEMENTS

To my readers: every review, every time you tell me you enjoyed my book is a blessing. Thank you to those of you who reached out to tell me what you thought. Thank you for letting me share my story and for continuing in this journey with me.

A huge thank you to everyone who helped me mold SHATTERED into a real book. My beta readers and CPs - I heart you guys big time.

Shout out to Craig Mason who provided me with invaluable advice on military Mishca.

She-Who-Must-Not-Be-Names...I miss your face. I will never forget that you pushed me into this journey with your demands for more Mishca and Ryder.

Sommies: I love that we are all still together. Thank you for the writing wars.

Aimee Salter and Marty Mayberry, you ladies have been my voice of sanity when I've needed it.

Sarah - thank you for sharing your love of bunnies and my love of cats. You have become such a great friend.

Toni - you wild party animal! Thanks for your support and insistence I dance even when wearing inappropriate shoes.

Heather - you are the best author assistant. I know I

don't show it enough, but you are just the bomb.

Emma - thank you for being an amazing web assistant. Your knowledge and willingness to help others astounds me.

Kate - thank you for putting up with my crazy flakiness and supporting me when I've needed it.

To my fellow YAtopians and Aussie Owned and Read gals, thanks for blogging with me.

Thank you Brenda Drake for letting me be part of the Pitch Wars Family. I love you. Thank you for being there for me through my crazy times. And thank you for giving me an excuse to visit America with The Pitch Wars Roadshow!

To my fellow PW mentors, I love the supportive community we've created. I treasure you all.

To my City Owl Press family, thank you for taking me under your wing and believing in me. Tina, your guidance is immeasurable. You haven't just made my writing better, but you've made me a better CP/ Beta for other writers. My fellow Owl authors, I appreciate the supportive group we've got. (Em, your hubby is hilarious).

My family - you put up with my absentmindedness when I'm in my writing cave haze, and yet, you've never stopped supporting my dream.

Hubby - Hey you. I love you, and I always will.

Your unwavering support of me pursuing my dreams is what I need. And thanks for the bike desk!

Ros - thanks for the emergency reads. I love your support. And thank you for Ryder's grammar joke.

Mum - you have been a rock for me. Thank you for your feedback and thank you for travelling around the world to support me. You definitely earned the title of Aussie Book Pimping Granny.

Thank you God for continuing to give me stories that embrace the weirdness that is me.

If I've forgotten to name you, know it's not intentional. I appreciate everyone who helps me on my journey.

ABOUT THE AUTHOR

SHARON M. JOHNSTON, from sunny Queensland, Australia, writes weird stories and soulful contemporaries. Working as a PR specialist by day, in her spare time she writes, blogs, plays with her fur babies, and enjoys computer games with her family. A regular host of Pitch Madness and a Pitch Wars mentor, a runner-up in The Australian Literary Review's short story competition, and a blogger with YAtopia and Aussie Owned & Read, she's a versatile artist. Well known for her sense of style, she's been stalked by women wanting to know where she buys her shoes.

www.sharonmjohnston.com